READERS LOVE FA
JACKIE K

HEALING GLASS

Healing Glass was one of those books that took me by surprise in an absolutely wonderful way. It's elegant and beautifully written and from page one it drew me in and kept me fully engaged. — Joyfully Jay

Gloriously and vividly crafted magical fantasy. — Mirrigold Reviews

I completely and utterly fell in love with the Warrior Guild. They are a band of brothers who go above and beyond. I was completely smitten. — Love Bytes Reviews

REPEAT OFFENCE

The tale made me jealous of a love without doubt or a time limit, even as the words built a terrible hunger in me for them to finally be together. — The Quille and Lampe

The author packed a world of despair, pain, hopelessness, heartbreak, darkness, and ultimately triumph, love, and an unexpectedly beautiful HEA ending into a short story guaranteed to keep you hooked long after you've turned the last page. — Repeat Offence, Patricia Nelson

SWORD OATH

Wonderful short intense story with miraculous choices and unconditional love from two beautiful passionate men who cannot live without each other. — Love Is Love Reviews

More Fantasy by Jackie Keswick

Gifted Guilds

Healing Glass
Embracing Fire (Coming Soon)

Dornost Saga Tales: Shades

Sword Oath
Shadow Realm
Soul Bound (coming soon)

Standalones

Repeat Offence
Baubles

CAUGHT

A BALANCE OF MAGIC, BOOK 1

JACKIE KESWICK

This is a work of fiction. Names, characters, places, and incidents either are the product of author imagination or are used fictitiously, and any resemblance to actual persons, living or dead, business establishments, events, or locales is entirely coincidental.

ISBN: 9798471977778

For Claire
Who believed that I could still do this.

PART 1
OTHERWORLD

GATHERING

Shimabara, Southern Japan, 22nd May 1792

The screams of the dying summoned Tenzen from his garden. He stepped through the veil into the human realm… straight into a puddle of cold, dirty water. More mud than water, he realised, yanking his boots free. The ground was a mix of sodden earth, splintered wood, sharp-edged shingles, and unidentifiable debris. Not a tree, not a house had remained standing. The city of Shimabara was gone, obliterated twice over.

Tenzen could read the signs. The mountain that had guarded Shimabara's back and had provided its bounty as long as people had lived here, now gaped like a hungry maw. Its flank had spilled out in a devastating rush of rock and rubble, burying half the town. Reaching the harbour, the slide had rolled on into the sea, creating a giant wave that wreaked havoc on the other side of the bay before returning to seal Shimabara's fate.

The dead numbered in the tens of thousands, and their screams had reached right into Tenzen's garden.

He turned his head from side to side, taking in the devastation. Salt spray stung his cheeks and the wind coming off the ocean tore his long hair out of its clasp. He gathered it with impatient fingers, twisting it into a tight braid.

Tenzen rarely needed to visit the human realm. Most souls recognised the time of their passing and came to him of their own accord. Here, though, death had taken thousands by surprise. Many had survived the landslide, only to fall to the giant waves a few hours later. Souls clustered above the destroyed town like blobs of dark smoke, confused and uncertain.

And already the predators circled high above.

Krull and hyeshi—minor demons who feasted on fresh souls. Souruita—who sought the souls of children to ensure their own youth and longevity. And the worst of all, rafeet, demons who thrived on fear and pain, who captured souls to torture them.

Shimabara drew them as a banquet would draw starving humans. And it was Tenzen's task to stop them.

His swords appeared in his hands, blades gleaming with purple fire. It proclaimed his status to everyone who saw him, souls and soul-eating demons alike.

There was no ideal place for this fight, no large space free of debris where he could move unimpeded. Tenzen's boots slipped on the treacherous footing made by loose soil and inches of water as he sought somewhat level ground.

He found it at the point where the landslide had reached the sea. There'd been no houses here, and the wall of rock and rubble had protected a small area from the worst of the wave. A few puddles dotted the ground, but Tenzen could move without tripping over roof beams or cooking pots or tangling his feet in netting or cloth.

He claimed his space and opened his mind, blades ready.

Souls rushed to him as their saviour, but so did the predators, sensing easy pickings. They swooped down, alone or in pairs, intent on snatching souls from the air, only to meet their end on his blades. It was messy, bloody work, but Tenzen soon found his stride, hacking and slashing, fighting for every soul that came to him.

It was not a task he'd chosen for himself, but even if he had, he would not have walked away from Shimabara.

For hours he gathered souls, while humans died around him. They breathed their last trapped under tons of rubble, perished from wounds and broken bones. Some succumbed to grief the moment they realised they'd lost everyone they'd had. Tenzen blocked their screams and sobs from his mind. He pictured his garden and focussed on his task with detachment and a steely determination that had served him before.

When darkness fell, fires bloomed on the rubble-strewn field that had once been a city. Survivors clustered around each one, unaware of the battle raging beside them, sharing what little food they'd scavenged from the devastation.

Instinct had sent them to the upper part of the city, close to the mountain that had laid waste to their town. It left Tenzen standing near the harbour, surrounded by the corpses of Otherworldly predators, and laden with souls to take back to his garden—not that any of the humans knew it. In the human realm, only the dead and the Yuvine could see him. And there were no Yuvine in Shimabara.

Tenzen shoved beheaded demons out of his way, cutting open their chests to destroy their hearts. Sweat, mud, and blood soaked him to the skin. Exhaustion numbed his limbs. Had he truly expected the Yuvine hunters to show? Or was his mind, weighed down with too many gathered souls, indulging in wishful thinking?

"Yamakage Jumon would have been here," he muttered to himself. It was true. The first Yuvine had never forgotten what it was like to be human. He'd worked for his gifts and didn't take them for granted. Not like his descendants who—

Quiet weeping met his ear. He scanned the area to his left and then his right and saw nothing but corpses and ruined houses. When he turned, however, he found a young woman, not much older than a girl, sitting amidst the wreckage. She curled over the lifeless body of a baby still in its crib, half buried under rubble. Beside her lay a young man, dead from a crushed skull. Their souls hovered close to the young woman, who was ashen under the layer of sticky mud.

Her soul scrabbled to free itself and Tenzen narrowed his eyes, intent to see past the wet, dirty dress that nearly hid her from view.

A blow to her middle had torn her spleen and liver. She was in pain, her abdomen filling with blood, and she already lacked the breath to cry out. Left as she was, she'd be dead by morning.

Tenzen stepped closer. She raised her eyes to his as if she sensed his presence, and Tenzen chose that moment to end her life so her soul could join those of her man and child.

Alerted now to the difficulty of spotting survivors, he walked the length of the harbour with his senses spread wide. But even after a second circuit, he found no more souls.

He bowed his head in respect and then parted the veil and returned to the Otherworld.

He stepped from deepest night into mid-morning, the early autumn mist all but burned off by the sun. Scents drifted on the breeze, a mix of damp soil, ripe apples, and a few late blooms.

Exhausted from the night's work and with his mind on his garden, Tenzen walked blindly through a curtain of shimmering grey tendrils. They clung to his hair and clothes and—with each step he took—they gathered closer, grew into strong ropes, and drew ever tighter… until they stopped Tenzen's progress and held him trapped.

HUNTING

Kiso Valley, Japan, eighteen years later

Rakurai set the delicate teacup onto the lacquer tray and let his gaze wander. When he'd arrived at the Yamakage Manor, a servant had conducted him to Yamakage Daisuke's private study—an opulent space of heavy mahogany furniture, gilded screens, and brush paintings adorning cream walls—rather than the audience hall where the elder usually held court and issued orders. It was as unprecedented a move as Daisuke's hesitancy in coming to the point.

Daisuke had already been head of the clan when Rakurai had come of age. And Daisuke's need to be obeyed without question had ensured they'd never grown close. They conducted their business in public, clan elder to designated clan hunter, and had never spoken in private.

Now Daisuke had welcomed him into his private domain and offered him tea. Then he'd talked endlessly about general clan affairs without telling Rakurai why he'd called for him. The change made Rakurai uneasy.

"And how is Raijin?" Daisuke asked before popping a cube of peach jelly into his mouth and daintily wiping his fingers on a napkin.

Rakurai kept his face blank. He loved his son, was fiercely proud of him, but it wouldn't do to show that sentiment too openly. "He's diligent in his studies and I'm satisfied with his progress."

It wasn't the whole truth. Raijin wielded lightning with a skill that belied his age, and Rakurai had begun to take him into the mountains to train. Another fact he had no intention to revealing just yet.

"Good. That's good. We need all our hunters, what with demon attacks increasing in both worlds. I'm hoping that Raijin will turn into as efficient a hunter as his father."

Rakurai ignored the compliment. Lightning wielders were rare amongst the twelve Yuvine clans, and those so gifted were always hunters. Of course, Daisuke wanted Raijin to be another such.

"Raijin is not yet of age," he reminded Daisuke. "It'll be years yet before he needs to choose his path. For now, I'm satisfied that he is showing promise."

Daisuke didn't ask how Rakurai himself was faring. Instead, he rambled on about the threat of demons to the human realm when Rakurai was sure that Daisuke had never faced a demon.

He let the words wash over him, unsure how he'd become Daisuke's confessor.

"…to tell you that we require the deaths of Ricci and Alyssa Lugano."

"What?" It was all the reply his shocked mind could devise. He pulled himself together and clarified: "You want me to kill two hunters from the Lugano clan? Two members of the Custodia?"

"They no longer serve in the Custodia," Daisuke hastened to reassure him. "Alyssa Lugano gave birth to a son a few years ago."

Rakurai waited because as explanations went, Daisuke's effort had been utterly inadequate.

Daisuke realised it, too, and flushed. "Alyssa has broken her bonding vows," he mumbled.

"How do you know this?"

"Their son looks nothing like his father."

Rakurai swallowed his retort. Bonding vows created an intimate connection between two Yuvine. If Alyssa Lugano had taken a lover, her bondmate would have known about it from the beginning. "Infidelity has never been a reason for a death sentence." Among the Yuvine, few things were. "Has Ricci Lugano requested the death of his mate?"

"Of course, Ricci did nothing of the sort!"

"Then why do you want me to kill them?" He didn't offer the respectful murmur of assent Daisuke expected. Instead, he kept pressing a matter Daisuke wanted dealt with quietly because everything in him revolted at the idea of killing two fellow Yuvine.

It seemed imprudent to reduce their numbers at a time when demon incursions were on the rise. And after having to watch Raijin deal with his mother's death, he was twice as reluctant to inflict such pain on another child without justification. "Forgive me, Elder. It doesn't make sense."

"The Luganos consorted with witches," Daisuke blurted out. "There you have it. The two consorted with witches and must die. You will see to it."

"I will not."

Daisuke's face grew redder. His mouth opened and closed without emitting any sound, until he resembled one of the koi he kept in his garden pond. "I have given you an order, Hunter. You will obey it."

"No. Have you forgotten Jumon's rule? *We do not involve ourselves in human politics and we do not kill each other.*" Rakurai quoted Yamakage Jumon, the first Yuvine and lawgiver. He'd made the rules they'd lived by for over ten thousand years. "I will not break Jumon's rules for your convenience. I will not kill other Yuvine unless in self-defence. And I will not be party to an unjustified murder."

Daisuke glared at him for what felt like hours. Rakurai made himself meet that stare without flinching. He watched Daisuke master his anger and wrap himself in his dignity as if it were a cloak. It was a fascinating display, but Rakurai wasn't entertained. Nor would it prompt him to change his mind. When Daisuke rose, he followed suit.

"You're not known for shirking your duties."

Rakurai stood his ground. "I will always do my work as a hunter. Killing other Yuvine was never part of a hunter's remit."

Daisuke's face transformed as a fresh wave of anger shredded his dignified façade. He drew himself up and glared. "If you can't follow orders, you're of no use to me, Yamakage Rakurai. Get out of my sight."

The Nakasendo, the route from Edo to Kyoto, teemed with traders and ordinary folk in search of entertainment. Many travellers had no other reason for being on the road than to admire the views as the season changed from a hot, humid summer to a cool, colourful autumn. Groups of fashionably dressed men and women clustered on bends and hilltops, chattering, sketching, and enjoying the clement weather.

Rakurai covered the ground with long, angry strides that sent travellers and animals scattering out of his way. He appeared like a grand lord's retainer and carried swords and whip in his belt, but the glances cast his way didn't hold fear. The gleaming white, silver-edged haori of the Yamakage hunters was a frequent sight on the

Nakasendo. And the travellers on the Shogun's highway had all heard the rumours.

It was Rakurai's third day on the road. He should talk to the merchants, the soldiers, and the casual travellers who shared his journey. Should find out what they'd seen of the demon he hunted.

If he'd believed this mission genuine, he might have done just that.

Problem was, he didn't believe it. Demon activity had increased of late. That much was true. But that a rafeet should hunt so close to Yamakage Manor, just after Rakurai had defied his clan elder... was too convenient.

Yamakage Daisuke was a snake. He craved status. And since he made it his business to know everyone else's concerns, revenge came easy to him. He knew that Rakurai watched over his son with eagle eyes. Knew that he'd increased his vigilance after Naomi's death. Forcing him to leave Raijin for a spurious mission was a punishment.

A fresh surge of anger heated Rakurai's blood, made his fingers itch for the grip of a sword or the handle of his whip. At any other time, he'd have enjoyed travelling while the trees changed into their autumn garb. Today, he took no notice of what lay to either side of the road. He barely saw anything travelling on it.

Yamakage Rakurai had lived for five hundred and eighty-four years. He was a hunter, skilled and conscientious, who didn't ignore a summons from the head of his clan. But he couldn't accede to Daisuke's request to kill two Lugano hunters.

He'd thrown Jumon's rule in Daisuke's face and had seen him flinch at the challenge. The Yuvine had their place in the worlds, and the rules laid down by Yamakage Jumon had served them for ten thousand years.

Until Daisuke found it acceptable to break them.

Rakurai didn't intend to follow Daisuke along that path but wondered whether his refusal was enough to halt Daisuke's plans. Should he have done more to persuade him? *Could* he have done more?

He'd been preparing to leave the Yamakage Manor—still undecided on that point—when a clerk had brought reports of a rafeet—a demon that thrived on fear and pain—terrorising the Kiso valley. The information was sketchy and contradictory. If the rafeet actually existed, the task of hunting and killing it would keep Rakurai from his home for weeks.

Daisuke wasn't a man to forget an insult.

And Rakurai had remembered it too late.

He slowed his angry march when he caught up with a trader and his troop halfway to the next post town. The men appeared nervous and shaken, more so than anyone else Rakurai had encountered in the last three days.

"We wanted to reach the market early, so we spent last night on the road," the trader told him. "We won't make that mistake again."

"What happened?"

"Nothing to us. But… the villagers tell tales of something slaughtering their livestock and driving men out of their minds with fear. Not that I've seen it. Or believed it. But last night… there's something in the forest just to the east that frightens all the creatures. Such screams we've heard!" He shuddered. "But not of things dying."

Rakurai nodded his thanks. "A demon who thrives on fear and pain. To the east, you said?"

The man turned to point up a narrow valley where the trees already wore the deep red of autumn, and an arrow missed his head with an inch to spare.

"Down!" Rakurai yelled at the man's retainers. He dragged the merchant to the ground, covering him with his body before shoving him into the shelter of a nearby tree.

He was up again in a heartbeat, sword and whip in hand, sprinting towards the bend in the road where the arrow had originated.

Other arrows came, but he dodged them.

By the time he'd rounded the bend and faced five men, his temper was blazing once more. An ambush on the busy Nakasendo road would be like a beacon to a demon who relished fear. If he didn't end this swiftly, he'd have to fight the creature while the humans watched. It wouldn't be the first time, but he much preferred to slay demons in the Otherworld.

The first two ambushers fell to his whip, the third one to his sword. The fourth showed a little more pluck and put up a fight. The fifth took to his heels. But not before Rakurai caught a glance of the man's face, which made him freeze where he stood.

The hesitation earned him a knife across the chest.

Rakurai hissed at the sting, jerking out of range of a follow-up slash. *Kuso!* Shit! Since when did anger make him careless?

He bit down on another curse and returned his mind to the fight. It took effort, because the man he'd seen fleeing the ambush scene had been none other than Yamato, Yamakage Daisuke's private secretary.

They left the bodies by the side of the road, the trader offering to report the ambush to the next Shogun's patrol. Rakurai let the man fuss over him, accepting linen to bandage the cut on his chest, and sake to dull the pain. He accompanied the troop until they were close enough to the next posting town. Then he retraced his steps to the ambush site and headed east up the valley where the merchant had noted the demon activity.

Along the way he found rabbits hanging from trees by their guts, and a deer left to die with deep wounds in its flank and its legs broken. Evidence of the rafeet sucking the last dregs of terror and suffering from its surroundings before it crossed back into the Otherworld.

The veil's sticky tendrils dragged on Rakurai's hair and clothes as he passed into the Otherworld, following where the rafeet led. Sated from its foray through the human world, it hadn't tried to hide its passing, but Rakurai stayed cautious. Rafeet were amongst the most dangerous creatures preying on the human realm, and if he wanted to kill it, Rakurai would need to take it unawares.

He walked through the mists, gaze scanning the trees and bushes lining the path. Judging by the colour of the leaves and the bounty of fruit, the seasons still aligned on both sides of the veil, though the time of day did not. He'd left the human realm in the late afternoon, yet here it appeared to be early morning. And something—or someone—called to him.

There were no words, just a powerful tug on his awareness. A tug that made him want to follow the path, walk faster, run—

He stopped.

Breathed.

The tug eased a fraction, but didn't disappear.

"Who are you and what do you want?"

The trees swallowed Rakurai's question and returned no answer. Could this be the rafeet's doing? Did it have the power to make Rakurai rush headlong into a trap? He'd never read of such a skill.

He took a careful step forward.

The tug eased a little more.

He took a step back the way he'd come.

The tug grew stronger.

"Understood," he said, irony strong in his voice. He had to find the rafeet, but he could spare some time to see what other creature had need of him.

He followed the path, watching the bark of the trees, the grass, and the rushes underfoot for signs of the rafeet's passing. There weren't any now. The demon wouldn't hunt on its own turf, and it would take care not to lead a hunter to its lair.

It grew warmer as Rakurai walked, and the sun had passed its zenith when he topped a ridge overlooking a manor house set in a neat pattern of fields. The dwelling looked much like his own: three wings of rooms arranged around a courtyard, dark wooden beams on foundations of rough stone, with a veranda edging each wing, and shoji screens hiding the interior from view.

Servants passed back and forth, and Rakurai saw people tending the fields. He thought about approaching openly, like a traveller looking for a place to rest, but finally dismissed the idea. Instead, he slept the afternoon away, up on his ridge, then slid through the fields under cover of dusk, found a sheltered spot beside the house, and waited for full darkness.

The statue in the courtyard had drawn him here, he realised as he began to explore. Shaped like a tall man with long flowing hair, it stood on a plinth surrounded by water. The artist had caught each swirl of robes and hair with precision, as if the figure walked in a light breeze and was just about to take the next step. It was an exceptional work, worthy of an emperor's court, and Rakurai wondered who had stolen it, and why.

He waited until a cloud dimmed the moonlight, then crossed the courtyard to get as close to the sculpture as he could.

The statue regarded him from glowing violet eyes, and the moment their gazes connected a voice, deep and commanding, rang in Rakurai's mind.

Get me out of here!

CAUGHT

Rakurai recoiled so hard he almost landed on his arse. He'd not had another's voice in his mind since Naomi's death, and the sudden command—and command it had been—came as a shock. He wrapped himself in mist, hoping to hide his hasty movements, and heard a chuckle.

I can still see you, Yuvine.

I wasn't hiding from you, Rakurai thought, using the same pathways he'd have used to talk to Naomi. It didn't feel as strange as he'd expected.

You don't need to try so hard, either. I'm not deaf.

What are you?

Can't you tell? The sculpture shot back, its eyes flashing violet.

Only death gods, Shinigami, had violet eyes. Rakurai had never met a death god. Or thought that they stood frozen on plinths, surrounded by water.

And then it all came together.

A demon trap.

Yes. The voice held so much sorrow that tears gathered in the corners of Rakurai's eyes. *It caught me as I was returning from a soul collection.*

Rakurai could fill in the rest for himself. If the Shinigami had gathered souls that had died in fear and pain, he'd have appeared like a walking banquet to the rafeet. *It wants the souls.*

It will not have them, the god said. *Even if it keeps me trapped here for the rest of my years. Are you hunting the rafeet?*

I am.

Then you can help me escape this prison and we can defeat it together.

Why would I do that?

Because if you try it alone, you will fail. This rafeet isn't like the others.

Rakurai hesitated. It was common knowledge that Shinigami valued truth and honour above all other traits. Despite that, his teachers had warned him to mistrust the gods and never to do their bidding.

Help me out of this trap and I will grant you a boon of your choosing, the Shinigami offered as if he had heard Rakurai's thoughts.

Rakurai stared into the glowing violet eyes and recalled the hint of mirth when the god had first spoken to him. Any being capable of mirth while caught in a rafeet's trap deserved his respect and his help. He drew a deep breath. *I am Yamakage Rakurai, hunter for the*

Custodia, he offered. And gathered all his courage. *Will you honour me with your name?*

The impression of a smile came to him first, comforting like a cool wash of summer rain on parched ground. Then the Shinigami's chuckle sent shivers rippling over Rakurai's skin.

You are a brave man, Yamakage Rakurai, to trust me with your name. Such bravery shall not go unrewarded.

Again, Rakurai felt the smile.

My name is Tenzen.

Rakurai bowed his respect. *Can we speak when I'm not standing in front of you?* The night was passing and soon the first of the manor's retainers would wake. It was a miracle that he'd been able to converse so long with the Shinigami without seeing a guard.

I've heard your mind's voice, Tenzen told him gravely. *I can find you. You are leaving?*

Withdrawing to a safe distance, Rakurai corrected, not liking the hint of accusation in Tenzen's mental voice. *I need to learn the area and study the rafeet's movements. I did not know that a rafeet could trap a god.*

An ordinary rafeet cannot, but have you noticed this manor? The people here are its puppets. The rafeet uses them to spin a web strong enough to compete with my power.

Something cold crawled down Rakurai's back. "Demonspawn," he whispered.

Accurate. Scores of them. Holding as many souls as I do right now, I can control, maybe, a handful of demonspawn at one time. That's not enough to unravel the net and open the trap.

I've read about demons that can turn humans into puppets, Rakurai said. *But a demon that can connect a group of enthralled individuals into an army, and make them act under its direction without a will of their own? That's remarkable.*

The rafeet doesn't just control their bodies, either. It binds their souls along with their minds and their spirits.

You have learned much.

I've had years to observe and ponder until I understood the nature of the trap holding me. I do not want to spend an equal number of years trying to work out a means to escape.

Years! The Shinigami had been trapped for years! Rakurai couldn't fathom such a fate. *Nor will you. I give you my word that I will not leave here without you.*

Then I will trust the word of a Yuvine.

Tenzen's voice held enough disbelief to raise Rakurai's hackles. Only the deep disquiet he sensed in the god's words made him keep his temper. *I'll find a safe place we can use as our base,* he said as he prepared to depart. *I will think about destroying the net the rafeet has woven around you. And I will keep speaking to you.*

The wave of warmth washing over him nearly took his breath. It felt like a promise and a caress, and it left Rakurai with a heart that beat a little too fast and a soul filled with unnamed longing. Was the god—Tenzen— using his magic to ensure Rakurai helped him escape the way he'd used his magic to bring Rakurai to his side? Rakurai didn't know and found that it didn't matter.

I promised you my help, he confirmed as he left. *I won't go back on my word.*

REMOTE SENSING

Tenzen's gaze followed the Yuvine until he passed from his sight. After that, he listened to Rakurai's mind, not caring that Rakurai's thoughts should have been his own. He'd been alone for too long, his only diversion the rafeet and its spawn.

Tenzen had little regard for the Custodia, the band of hunters formed to fulfil their clans' obligation to defend the two worlds against the darkness. Once, they'd been diligent in their duties, policing the veil and fighting demons. But that diligence had dwindled over the years, leaving demons to ravage both worlds almost unopposed.

Yamakage Rakurai had admitted to serving in the Custodia, yet he differed from the other Yuvine who'd hunted the rafeet. Not one of them had cared about the rafeet's spawn or its unwilling victim. The last, Vigdis Perkhon, the senior hunter for the second oldest Yuvine clan, had even dared to mock Tenzen before he turned his back on him and his plight.

Rakurai's hair was of a similar pale shade, and he wore it tied at the nape the way the Perkhon hunter had worn his. The similarities ended there. Vigdis's every movement had shown his disdain for his task, while Rakurai carried himself with an unconscious grace that would make him a joy to watch when he fought. Tenzen imagined it, pictured Rakurai traversing the grounds of the manor, slaying demonspawn to weaken the net until Tenzen could break free of it.

You really would not kill the demonspawn? The desire to hear another's voice after his long, lonely incarceration overrode the wish not to distract the hunter from his task. Or admit that he'd been listening to Rakurai's thoughts.

Their only crime has been to let the rafeet catch them, Rakurai said. *For that, I'd put no one to death. If they're no longer alive, of course, then it would be heartless not to end their existence.*

Do you always consider your decisions so carefully?

That's not something I claim. I aim to, but I'm no god.

Do you perchance think the gods are that considered? Tenzen found a good deal of amusement in their exchange. He was old—only three other gods in the two worlds were older—but he wouldn't claim that he weighed each of his decisions. Nor had he done so when he'd been younger. *If all my moves were that well thought out, I would not find myself in this predicament. My mind was on other things as I entered the rafeet's domain. Maybe I expected the rafeet to respect what I am. But demons let their instincts rule them, and I should have remembered that.*

Show me the man who never made a mistake and I'll show you a man who died before birth, Rakurai quoted, and Tenzen came as close to laughing as he had since the night he'd walked into the trap.

I apologise for distracting you, he said, truthful and not so truthful all at once.

Rakurai did not reply in words, but Tenzen sensed his smile as if the Yuvine was directing it at him.

He knew of the Yamakage, of course. The rise of the first Yuvine clan had been a sensation—the first time both their worlds had connected in the way Creation had intended. They'd all seen it as a new beginning, despite the trouble they knew would grow from the union.

He remembered Yamakage Jumon, an insightful, gifted shaman. He'd been a proud man with a regal bearing and eyes as dark as Rakurai's.

Attempting a spirit walk, he'd found his way to the Otherworld. His delight, when he'd realised his achievement, had touched them all. Even the Unseen Power, who'd agreed to a bargain with Jumon.

When Jumon had returned to the human realm, he'd created the Yuvine by sharing the celestial magic he'd been granted by the Unseen Power. Then he'd made the rules the Yuvine lived by. And while he wielded vastly more power than anyone, he'd abided by the rules he'd set until his last day.

On Jumon's death, Tenzen had gathered his soul with great care, nourishing it in his garden before sending it on its journey.

The Yamakage who came after had been men of lesser spirit. They cleaved to honour, but over time forgot its meaning. Now and then a Yamakage resembled the Yuvine of old, but there had been no one like Jumon for a few lifetimes.

Tenzen pushed the thoughts aside. It wasn't fair to lay such a burden on Yamakage Rakurai, a man he didn't know. Not even in thought, because thoughts held power.

His own stoic acceptance of the situation had disappeared the moment Rakurai had answered his call. Hope had taken its place, along with a curiosity he'd not felt in centuries.

Tenzen could no more stop observing the Yuvine than he could fly, imprisoned as he was.

At the manor's boundary Rakurai traded stealth for speed and followed the path into the woods despite a strange reluctance to leave. It was an uncomfortable sensation he'd only ever experienced over Raijin.

Do you sleep? He enquired as he sought shelter from the morning sun under the canopy of trees, wanting both an answer and to hear Tenzen's voice again.

The contact between them differed from what he'd shared with Naomi. They'd grown up together, had been friends long before they'd decided to be bonded, and their connection had been as comfortable as a soft blanket on a chilly night. Talking to Tenzen felt warmer, closer, but at the same time more exhilarating. And it drew him like light drew a moth.

I've not slept since the rafeet caught me. Tenzen's voice was a low rumble in the back of Rakurai's mind. *I do not trust him not to take the souls I guard by force should he find me less than watchful.*

The Shinigami was stubborn, but his adherence to his duty appealed to Rakurai. The rafeet might have freed him years ago had he given up the souls he guarded, but Tenzen had kept them safe and paid the price. *But in the ordinary course of things, you would sleep?*

Less than a human or Yuvine. But yes, I would sleep.

How about food?

Do not… ask about food. I beg of you.

This time, the sound in Rakurai's mind was a groan. With it came the impression of a gnawing hunger, stronger than anything Rakurai had ever felt. He added time to sleep, and food—a lot of food—to his plans. And then he realised he didn't know what kind of food a Shinigami liked. Or required.

I've never met a death god, he said. *I need to ask questions if I want to avoid insulting you.* Not to mention that Raijin would want to know every single detail, and would no doubt pose questions that had never occurred to Rakurai.

Neither your questions nor your ignorance will insult me. The air sustains me enough to keep me alive. Eating food is… a supplement. And a pleasant diversion I've been denied for far too long. Like moving.

You only have to endure it for a little while longer.

How is it that you are so different from the others of your kind?

Tenzen seemed just as eager for conversation, and Rakurai didn't mind answering, even when the question made little sense to him. *Different how?*

You're not the first Yuvine who found me in my prison. Those who came before you walked away, leaving me trapped and the rafeet unslain.

They came to hunt and left their task undone?

The rafeet still lives.

That's despicable conduct. Who were they? Rakurai wanted to make it his task to teach them a lesson— preferably a long and painful one.

You can leave them to me, Tenzen said. *I know who they are, and they'll find the end of their lives not as they expect.*

Rakurai shivered at the threat of retribution in Tenzen's mental voice. It was never wise to anger a god. Or to disappoint one.

He traversed the forest until he reached the roots of the mountain range that edged the valley. Turning to follow the line of hills, he searched for waterfalls, until he found one whose flow had carved out a sizable cave behind a curtain of water.

I've found a cave, he told Tenzen. *Let me see if it's suitable.*

The space behind the waterfall was high enough for Rakurai to stand upright, and wide enough for two men to stretch out without getting soaked by the fall. Moss covered the floor in big, pillowy hummocks, inviting him to rest his tired body. Best of all, though, water welled in a stone basin at the back of the cave. It steamed gently, and when Rakurai dipped his fingers in, he found it pleasantly hot. Maybe once he'd freed Tenzen, they could share this boon like two patrons at an onsen.

The thought made Rakurai's skin tingle and his prick harden. The reaction startled him. He'd only seen the statue the rafeet had turned Tenzen into. Had only heard Tenzen's voice in his mind. Why would—?

I feel your alarm. What is wrong? Tenzen queried.

Rakurai couldn't explain what he felt. He hadn't shared a sleeping mat with anyone but Naomi in two hundred years. Had not felt drawn to another man in far longer than that. And Tenzen was a death god, bound to the Otherworld, with duties and tasks Rakurai knew nothing about.

The novelty of the situation was responsible for his wayward feelings, he decided. Talking mind to mind, the way he would have done with Naomi, had tinted compassion with desire.

He wouldn't mention that. Neither was he going to reveal that he'd found a hot spring. The hunger and longing emanating from Tenzen when he'd asked about food had been impossible to ignore. He wouldn't taunt him with visions of a steaming bath when the chance of enjoying one was still days away.

Rakurai?

Nothing's wrong. The cave is roomy enough for the two of us to sleep. He didn't wait for Tenzen's answer, asking questions to silence his own mind. *Has nobody missed you all these years? Has nobody missed the souls you carry? Or are you the only Shinigami?*

There are seven of us. We're spread wide across the two worlds. We meet and speak only rarely.

What a lonely existence. Rakurai shivered. He spent much of his time alone, but nothing like—

I relish solitude, Rakurai. All death gods do. It's one thing that made my confinement—

Don't you dare say easy to bear!

That chuckle again. *I won't. And I apologise for listening to your thoughts.*

You should, Rakurai said lightly, even though his cheeks burned. *Listeners at doors rarely hear good things.*

This time, Tenzen's mental voice was a genuine laugh. *You talk to me, and you've found a cave. I've no complaints so far.*

FREED

Eighteen years hadn't been long enough to change the view. Tenzen stared past the far reaches of the courtyard to the fields and the river. A light breeze swayed the trees, while their leaves, not yet touched by autumn, rustled and changed colour from deep green to silver. Rice fields rose in terraces up the side of the ridge. The orchard lay straight ahead, and plots for vegetables and grain hugged the bends of the river.

Tenzen had watched the seasons come and go, unable to react to anything he saw. And now he trusted a Yuvine to help him change that?

I'm in position.

Had Tenzen been able to move, he would have sagged in relief. For two days and nights, while Rakurai planned and prepared as was the way of the Yuvine hunters, they'd talked about everything and nothing. Tenzen had found the Yuvine conscientious, compassionate, honourable…yet he'd not truly believed that Rakurai would return to the manor to help him escape the rafeet's trap. Now Rakurai was proving him wrong, and Tenzen didn't want to admit his doubts. But there was something he could and should say.

Thank you.

Thank me when we have you out of there. Tension roughened Rakurai's voice. He'd concocted a paralysing draught, deeming it the fastest method to disable the demonspawn. Then he'd decided on the time the workers left the fields and returned to the manor for their evening meal as the best time to catch them unawares.

I've used this before, on a possessed soul, he told Tenzen. *Once its puppet could not move, the demon left her body. Maybe, with so many spawn to control, disabling them will—*

For the moment, Tenzen didn't care what happened to the rafeet or its spawn. He wanted out of this trap. And Rakurai, as promised, lay hidden in the bushes lining the path, blowpipe at the ready, waiting for the workers to head home.

What's taking so long?

Your anticipation, Rakurai chuckled. Then, as if to add insult to injury, he added a soothing, *Not long now.*

Tenzen gritted his teeth. His helplessness grated, more than it ever had in the last eighteen years. He'd tried not to let himself hope, knowing how callous the Yuvine could be. Only... Rakurai wasn't like the others.

His character held honour and compassion in equal measure. And Tenzen had begun to believe that—

They're past me, Rakurai said, and Tenzen imagined him rising to his full height. *Brace.*

Tenzen counted eight beats of his heart one by one while he waited for the column of workers to come into view.

As Rakurai's darts hit, the rafeet's minions dropped one after the other. The pressure binding Tenzen's powers lightened by degrees. He knew he should wait, should husband his strength and concentrate it for one mighty push... but years of being trapped unmoving like a fly in amber made him desperate.

Tenzen poked and shoved at the strands of the net, trying to loosen its hold, and paying only scant attention to Rakurai's race through the manor.

The final three demonspawn fell to Rakurai's darts. The net gave way, and Tenzen swayed on the plinth.

He'd made a mistake.

After years of imprisonment, his legs would not bear his weight. And caring for the souls he carried took his remaining strength.

He remembered the rafeet boasting about the cost of installing the basin of poisoned water, the demon's assertion that, after a few years trapped in the net, he'd no longer have the strength to jump its width. Unless he kept his balance, he would drown in the murky liquid and—

A bolt of lightning split the edge of the water basin.

The poisoned sludge poured out and soaked the gravel, just as Rakurai's shoulder hit his middle. The impact catapulted him backwards off the plinth, away from the wet stones, and past the opposite rim of the basin.

They landed with a thud.

Tenzen felt solid earth under his back, Rakurai's weight on top of him, and the touch of fresh air on his cheeks. It was almost too much.

"Thank you," he said, throat raw as if he'd swallowed splinters. "Rakurai," he tried again. Only for a coughing fit to rip through his chest.

"Here." Rakurai braced himself on one elbow and offered Tenzen a small flask. "I brought water."

He shifted to the side. Tenzen pushed himself to sitting, took the flask, and gulped the contents. The flask was metal, which explained why it hadn't broken when they'd landed. And why the water tasted so strange.

His hand shook and his weakness shamed him. He was a god, and yet he barely had the strength to stand on his own. He guarded the souls in his keeping with nothing but stubbornness.

"Thank you," he said once more. His throat was just as raw as before, but at least he had a voice again.

He struggled upright, clinging to Rakurai and swaying like a sapling in a storm.

Rakurai didn't suggest he carry him. He wrapped an arm around Tenzen's waist and pulled Tenzen's other arm over his shoulder, offering as much support as

Tenzen was willing to take as they skirted the broken basin and the damp patches of poison soaking the ground.

"I don't know whether the rafeet felt me disabling his spawn."

"Then we'd better leave. I'm in no shape just yet to confront a rafeet. And I don't want to leave you fighting by yourself."

Every muscle in Tenzen's body screamed as he placed one foot in front of the other. His breath sawed in and out like bellows, and his stomach, woken from the paralysis, added to his discomfort.

He didn't complain.

The agonies were nothing but proof that he'd escaped the rafeet's trap and was free to take his revenge as soon as he'd recovered his strength.

And that trusting Yamakage Rakurai had been a well-considered decision.

Screams and the sound of rushing water roused Tenzen from sleep. Eyes screwed shut and breathing rapid, he checked the souls he held. Nothing had harmed them while he slept, and Tenzen relaxed by cautious degrees. He'd escaped the rafeet's trap, but until he reached his garden the souls remained in danger. The thought rankled. In all his years gathering souls, no demon had ever caught him. But a harvest like Shimabara was a rare event.

Dreams had woken him, he realised. Blood-soaked nightmares of the day before his capture, when he'd fought for every single soul in that devastated city. And then he'd dreamed of thirst, and hunger, and being held unmoving. The rafeet's taunting laughter. His own stubborn refusals.

Refusal to surrender the souls he carried, to sleep, or let discomfort and repeated Yuvine betrayals move him from his path.

Rakurai's arrival at the rafeet's manor had multiplied his battles. He'd needed to steel himself to ask for help, then had to fight against the cautious hope that grew with every conversation he'd shared with the Yuvine. Keeping the growing trust at bay had been exhausting, but Rakurai had proved himself. And now…

Tenzen blinked through the last remaining tendrils of his dreams.

He'd been as weak as a piece of wet rope once the rafeet's trap had let him go. Rakurai had plied him with sips of a potent spirit to get him over the last few miles, his apologetic grimace making it clear that he'd prefer to have carried Tenzen.

But he'd not offered, and Tenzen had not asked.

Tenzen had drunk the spirit and called on all of his millennia-old cussedness to make it to their shelter.

He'd wanted to talk to Rakurai, learn more about the unusual Yuvine, plan their attack. Instead, he'd managed a single cup of weak tea before exhaustion had claimed him. Now his stomach's grumbling made him think that food might not be out of the question.

He rolled to his side and rose to his knees, swaying as dizziness assaulted him.

Yes, food would be marvellous.

He turned his head from side to side, scanning the small cave. It was all but hidden behind the fall of the water. Moss framed the entrance and carpeted the cave's floor. Of Rakurai there was no sign.

Rakurai?

I'm hunting for food. I left tea and rice cakes for you.

Tenzen didn't reply with words, but he sent a wave of warmth and gratitude to Rakurai. He remembered encouraging words, a sturdy shoulder, and a comforting grip when he faltered. And lightning. He remembered the lightning that had split the basin of poisoned water and the tackle that had saved him from a fall.

Tenzen drank the tea and then reached for the stack of rice cakes. They were senbei, crisp bites with a sweet-salty glaze that made his mouth water. He ate the topmost one, and his hunger grew into a ravenous beast that wanted to devour the entire stack at once. He rationed himself, sipping the cold, sweet tea, and waited for his body to adjust.

It was fortunate that gods didn't waste away like starving humans did, or eighteen years of captivity would have turned him into a skeleton. At least the air had kept him alive.

Even if it hadn't been much of a life.

He pushed the thought aside, deciding that he had more important things to think about. Like Rakurai by himself and in reach of the rafeet.

How far did you go?

Not far. I'm already on the way back. Try to sleep.

Rakurai wasn't lying. His presence drew nearer. Tenzen's eyes closed without his permission, and he sank down onto his pallet of moss, mind on Rakurai as he drifted off to sleep once more.

Sacrifice

Tenzen slept peacefully on his pillows of moss when Rakurai ducked around the waterfall. Relief was instantaneous, as if he'd expected to find the Shinigami missing on his return.

The sculpture in the rafeet's manor, gorgeous though it had been, hadn't done him justice. Rakurai contemplated Tenzen's creamy skin, the long silky strands of raven hair, the perfectly shaped mouth, and the delicate hands and feet. The only imperfection was the lashes that lay, just a touch too long, like fans against Tenzen's cheeks.

Tenzen had struggled to keep his feet on their dash from the rafeet's manor, but he was as stubborn as he was beautiful.

With his eyes closed, he appeared less godlike. His brows drew together as if he concentrated on a difficult task, but the hours of sleep had smoothed the lines of exhaustion that had bracketed his mouth.

Tenzen's lips stirred want deep in Rakurai's gut. What he'd labelled as desire-tinged compassion had grown stronger while he'd watched Tenzen sleep. And a wave of confusion had built in its wake.

He barely remembered wanting another man. And who'd ever heard of a Yuvine lusting after a god? All the stories he knew had told of death gods lusting after mortals—even long-lived ones like the Yuvine—as if they craved that touch of impermanence to leaven their immortality.

Did he, after losing his parents and Naomi, desire immortality to steady his shifting world? And was a death god the kind of immortal to give him what he sought?

Rakurai pushed to his feet and returned to the bag he'd left at the cave entrance. He knew what he was doing: pondering unsolvable riddles to distract himself from uncomfortable feelings. Like finding a Shinigami attractive and not knowing what to do about it.

Focus on survival, he reminded himself. *We have a rafeet to kill.*

He stirred the embers of the small fire back to life before he heated water for tea. He'd snared a rabbit and collected wild herbs and now set about making soup. He knew little about the way gods reacted to starvation—had he even known that gods could starve?—but a rich, soothing broth would—

It smells fabulous, Tenzen purred into his mind, causing ripples of goosebumps on Rakurai's skin. *I am grateful for your care.*

Rakurai flushed. Tenzen's remark, coming right when he was thinking about—

"Can you hear every one of my thoughts?"

"No. Yes." This time, Tenzen spoke. And while his voice was still dry and raspy, the attempt didn't leave him hacking up a lung.

"No or yes?"

"Both, actually. I can choose to listen to your mind at will, but I try to respect your privacy. If you speak, however, I cannot help hearing the thoughts connected to your words, and the intent behind them. You were muttering under your breath as you stirred the broth, so I heard you wonder whether broth would appeal to me. The answer is yes, broth sounds wonderful!"

Rakurai breathed a little easier. He'd not been aware of talking to himself, but… it wasn't outside the realm of possibility. "Would you like to try my broth?" He asked to distract himself.

"I would." Tenzen pushed himself upright and sat, blinking those gorgeous eyes of his, like a cat woken from a nap.

"Dizzy?"

"Yes. I hoped it would pass."

"You need to eat." Rakurai spooned broth into a bowl and handed it to Tenzen, watching him devour the soup. "There's more," he said, when Tenzen handed the empty bowl back. "But you need to give your body time to adjust."

"You appear to have experience in this field."

"I've served as a hunter all my adult life and I've rescued my share of prisoners over the years." He made himself face Tenzen's violet gaze despite the butterflies that whirled in his gut. "I understand human needs, but what does a death god need to recover? What do you need?"

"Food will help," Tenzen said. "As I said, it's usually an indulgence, since the air in the Otherworld sustains me."

"This is why you didn't perish."

"Yes. But I couldn't use it to its fullest extent, trapped as I was."

"So food and... time?"

"Magic," Tenzen added. "To regain all my strength, I also require magic."

Rakurai considered that. Every living thing held magic, and the Otherworld practically thrummed with it, but... "How does a god absorb magic?"

Tenzen's lips quirked as if the question amused him. "Killing the rafeet will provide more than I have need of. But I don't dare go up against it without at least some of my powers restored. Which creates rather a conundrum for me."

"Can you take power from me? Without killing me, I mean."

"All gods can draw power from living creatures."

"No doubt, but you said you needed to kill to release that power."

"I don't *need* to kill. I'm a death god, Rakurai. I care for souls. I wouldn't harm a soul whether it is in my keeping or still in its host body."

Tenzen seemed taller all of a sudden, more god-like. Shadows shrouded his form and his eyes glowed an unearthly violet. He was utterly compelling, and Rakurai shivered.

"If you took too much magic, you'd harm my soul?"

"Draining too much of its magic harms a soul, yes. So does draining magic without consent." The shadows disappeared and Tenzen took a second bowl of broth from Rakurai's hand. "Draining a soul's magic without its consent is why most demons, along with succubi and incubi, fall under the hunters' remit," he said when he'd drained the bowl. "Do the Yuvine no longer teach these truths?"

"They did not teach us about souls," Rakurai admitted. "Not beyond the fact that we each have them." Tenzen's disgusted moue made him chuckle. "This is, perhaps, a discussion for another day. If you're reluctant to take my magic… how about gifts? Is there a way I can share my lightning with you? Would it help restore you?"

"Of course."

"What must I do?"

"Wait." Tenzen hadn't changed his serious demeanour. "I don't want you to offer out of ignorance.

If you share your lightning with me, that ability will forever remain with me. How comfortable are you with leaving a death god able to wield lightning?"

Heat darkened Rakurai's cheeks and neck, and he prayed that Tenzen *wouldn't* read his thoughts. He'd offered his help in good faith, but Tenzen's question had more than unsettled him. Tenzen had no need for additional lightning-wielding skills. He unleashed lightning every time they spoke mind to mind.

"Rakurai?"

He raised his gaze to meet Tenzen's, and the air filled with static, crackling and alive as if a thunderstorm was close.

"Will it diminish my ability? Make me less effective as a hunter?" He thought of Raijin, back in their home at his lessons, and the longing to see him was all-encompassing. "I have a son," he admitted. "I don't want to jeopardise my chance to see him grow into a hunter."

Tenzen's gaze darkened to a deep, mysterious purple, and Rakurai felt his regard like a physical touch.

"If you share your lightning with me, there will be no negative effects. This is a promise," he said.

Rakurai believed him without question. "What must I do?"

"Hit me with a lightning bolt. Preferably away from all this running water."

They found an open patch of grass at a decent distance from the river. As soon as he'd surveyed the area and declared it suitable, Tenzen sank to the ground with a sigh and folded his legs beneath him. "The sooner I no longer feel like an old man, the better it will be."

"Compared to me, you *are* an old man." Rakurai waited for Tenzen's smile. It was becoming quite ridiculous how much he craved the Shinigami's smile and the warm tone of his voice.

Tenzen obliged with a quirk of his lips. "I'm an old man compared to almost everyone," he said. "Most years, the advantages and limitations balance themselves."

Rakurai didn't want to imagine Tenzen alone for millennia before the mortals understood their magic, and still alone after they had forsaken all their gifts. Living this way must take a great deal of strength, and it explained Tenzen's frustration at having to face his life's challenges without his accustomed abilities. "Tell me what to do to help restore your powers."

Tenzen's half-smile morphed into something impish that reminded Rakurai of playing pranks as a child.

"Hit me with a lightning bolt," he repeated his earlier words.

Rakurai raised a hand and called the lightning.

The bolt hit Tenzen square in the chest. His head snapped back, and his long hair fanned out as if a strong breeze lifted and spread it. From one moment to the next, he looked frozen, suspended, speared by lightning like a sacrifice.

Gifted to him first at birth and then, once more, at his naming, lightning was as familiar to Rakurai as breathing. Aware that its power was vast but fleeting and a misstep could have dire consequences, Rakurai wielded it with respect.

He never forgot that lightning was a balance, that—born from the powers of air and earth—it linked the two for the briefest of moments.

Not this time.

The sweet, pungent scent of lightning-struck air filled the clearing as Rakurai's lightning bolt became a glowing rope connecting him to Tenzen. It arced across the meadow, changing from blinding white to purple to midnight blue, until Rakurai felt a tug deep in his gut. Something inside him gave, like a long unused door swinging wide, and then his strength poured out of him, along the rope, and into Tenzen.

It was an uncanny feeling, but not exactly painful. Rakurai didn't fight it. He opened himself to the sensation and embraced the lassitude that seemed to come in its wake.

The clearing faded from his view.

Sounds receded.

Only the scent of lightning remained, the glow of the rope, and Tenzen, whose smile was of such singular sweetness that Rakurai couldn't tear his gaze away.

Tenzen's smile brought a wash of joy, a brightness that enveloped Rakurai from head to foot, that warmed and soothed, and left contentment and peace when it faded.

BARGAIN

The lightning bolt hit his chest like a giant fist. It didn't hurt, but the force snapped his head back so hard Tenzen saw stars. Heat sizzled through him, driving out the cold of starvation and despair. He welcomed the burn, the scouring of old memories. It made room for the wash of power that followed the blast of heat—a rush so sweet it made him gasp in relief. His starving cells soaked up every bit of nourishment, filling and plumping and healing.

He opened his eyes to find Rakurai a few feet away, clinging to the lightning as if it were a rope—a glowing rope that turned from white to purple to deep blue as Tenzen soaked up power.

Rakurai's power.

Another wave of strength reached him; sweeter and even more potent. It brought euphoria, the wish to dance and sing and scream and re-arrange the world to his liking.

This feeling he knew. It was the magic inherent in all things.

Alarm tingled down his spine. Rakurai had offered to share the power of his lightning. He wasn't supposed to give his magic. Not the magic in his soul.

"Let go! Rakurai! Drop the lightning!" He was already on his feet when Rakurai toppled like a felled tree.

The glowing rope stuck to them as if determined to keep them joined. As if it had a mind of its own and that mind wanted to see Rakurai dead.

Tenzen wouldn't allow it.

He grabbed the lightning with both hands and yanked. Bolts of heat shot through him, making him dizzy. Did Rakurai feel like that when he used his gift? Dizzy, euphoric, wanting to burn the world to ashes? When the glowing rope finally came free, Tenzen felt as if he'd torn out his own heart. But finally… finally… the lightning's glow faded into nothing.

"Rakurai! Talk to me!"

He fell to his knees beside Rakurai, turned him over with gentle hands.

Rakurai's skin was paler than his silver hair, his blue-tinged lips the only splash of colour. He wasn't breathing. But the smile on his face was more beautiful than the sunrise over Tenzen's garden. Wherever Rakurai was going, he wasn't afraid.

"Rakurai, no! I command you to stay! This is not your time."

He swept the unconscious Yuvine into his arms and raced for the cave. This was not meant to happen. He'd promised that no harm would come to Rakurai.

He ducked around the waterfall, tripped on a pillow of moss and almost dropped his burden.

"This. Is. Wrong!" He grated the words through his teeth as he settled Rakurai onto the moss. The wash of euphoria had congealed into shivery fear. "This is wrong. I *promised*. This cannot happen."

Rakurai didn't respond, and Tenzen cradled his face in his hands, breathed across his lips.

Nothing.

"Idiotic. Uncaring. Overzealous. Liar…" That last thought stopped him. He'd believed that Rakurai wanted to see his son grow. But what if—No. Rakurai had been serious. Genuine.

"Help me," he pleaded with the Unseen Power that ruled all living things. "Help me. It is not his time."

He cradled Rakurai's cheek, the skin still warm and soft, without the lifeless waxiness that came with death. Even narrowing his focus, he couldn't see Rakurai's soul. Maybe—

Misadventure. The disembodied voice rang through his mind. *Misadventure.*

Tenzen shuddered. Clutched at Rakurai as if he could anchor him to this life. "No! Please reconsider," he pleaded. "Yamakage Rakurai must live. I promised!"

You want to bargain?

No death god ever wanted to hear those words. Shinigami rarely made promises, because breaking a promise had dire consequences. But bargains made with the Unseen Power were costly in ways none of them could imagine. Tenzen knew of the Shinigami who'd given his entire garden to save one human woman only to watch her die three months later in an accident. He'd avoided striking bargains in all his years, because it would never be him who bore the cost.

He ran his fingers through Rakurai's hair, over and over, as he memorised Rakurai's smile, remembered his kindness.

In eighteen long years, four Yuvine hunters had turned their backs on him. Rakurai had been the exception. Maybe his sense of duty hadn't allowed it. But why had he offered his gift to help restore Tenzen's powers? And what had prompted him to cling to the lightning and give all of himself to Tenzen?

Tenzen didn't have answers to his questions. He couldn't accept Rakurai's sacrifice if he didn't understand it.

"I want to bargain."

The silence was deafening. It draped the cave like a shroud, muting even the roar of the waterfall. Tenzen cradled Rakurai and waited, trying not to second-guess decisions he couldn't control. Rakurai felt right in his arms, solid and warm and as if he belonged there, when nothing and nobody had ever belonged to Tenzen before.

The realisation staggered him.

Rakurai was his.

That was the reason he'd asked for a bargain, even if he wouldn't know until the time came what the Unseen Power would demand of him.

And as if the Unseen Power had waited for him to understand this, the air in the cave suddenly shimmered and hummed.

If you can persuade him off the bridge, the bargain will stand.

Tenzen bowed his head and cradled Rakurai against his chest. His mind drowned in a mix of gratitude and fear that left him shaking. The Unseen Power hadn't solved his problem. Instead, he'd been offered a chance to save Rakurai.

This time, when he narrowed his eyes, he saw Rakurai's soul.

He reached for it, cradled it in his palm, and prepared to argue.

KISSED

Sounds of rushing water blended with a low rumble that resolved into angry mutterings the moment Rakurai concentrated. Tenzen's voice, he thought, and—

O kami, Tenzen!

Rakurai's eyes flew open.

And closed again in confusion.

They'd been in the meadow a little way from the river. How had he ended up back in the cave, stretched out on the pallet of moss and with Tenzen's anxious face leaning over him?

"Rakurai! Open your eyes and look at me!"

Rakurai winced at the strident tone.

"Rakurai!"

He opened his eyes. The cave walls rippled like bedsheets hung to dry, and his stomach roiled at the sight. He screwed his eyes shut and breathed through his nose, grateful that the buzzing in his head was loud enough to drown out Tenzen's anger.

His memories weren't just hazy, they were missing.

And the burning tingles in his limbs weren't fading the way pins and needles usually did once he started moving.

He scraped enough awareness together to voice a question. "What happened?"

Tenzen's fingers tightened on his. "You came too damned close to dying. Why didn't you let go of the lightning bolt?"

"What?"

"You clung to the lightning after you struck me. It stayed connected to both of us, draining your power until you collapsed. And you still wouldn't let go! Why didn't you?"

Rakurai had no answer, but at least Tenzen's words recalled the event to his mind. The lightning arcing from his palm to Tenzen's chest, the blazing white light turning first purple and then midnight blue. And the emotions surging through him...

Euphoric.

Peaceful.

Content.

None of those words described Rakurai's life, but if this was what his next life offered, he would go gladly.

He felt moisture gather on his lashes and blinked it away. Tenzen's gorgeous eyes gazed down into his, and Rakurai thought he understood. "That's what you do, isn't it? You comfort souls on their way to their next life. That's what you did for me."

Tenzen reared back as if Rakurai had struck him. "I did not! I promised that I wouldn't harm you, and you almost made me break my word."

"Oh. I... Please forgive me. But..." He'd meant to thank Tenzen for easing his path to the next life, but the expression on the Shinigami's face stopped him cold. Tenzen wasn't angry as he'd first thought. He was... afraid? Disappointed?

"Why Rakurai? I believed you when you said you wanted to see your son grow up."

Rakurai went cold. "I want that. Raijin is..." He licked his lips, tried to make sense of what had happened. Tried to understand why, in that wash of emotion, he hadn't thought of his son, when thoughts of Raijin had driven so many of his decisions in the last century. "We were... You need your powers so we can kill the rafeet. And I... Tenzen, I've never sought death. Not in battle, not when I grieved for my parents and my bondmate. Never. I wouldn't do that to my son."

Tenzen's gaze softened. His fingers found their way into Rakurai's hair, and he combed the strands with long, careful strokes. "Then what happened?"

The touch soothed Rakurai's agitation. "I don't know. No lightning has ever clung to me like this one did. Yuvine don't study for their gifts, you know? We gain them at birth and spend our lives learning to master them. But mastering lightning involves calling it, directing it where I want it to go, and to temper its power so I don't exhaust myself. It's a whip, Tenzen. Lightning is a whip, not a bridge."

"Between us, a bridge is what it became." The troubled expression returned to Tenzen's face. "You gave me your magic. Maybe I offered you comfort and ease. All I know is that you were crossing the bridge and bringing you back took some bargaining."

His gaze clouded further and Rakurai didn't think he should ask about that bargain. He focused on the present instead and calibrated his senses.

The rushing of the water.

The colour of the rock.

The touch of the moss on his skin.

The taste of something green and bitter on his lips.

"I'm buzzing," he said when he'd convinced himself that he would live.

"I hope that will pass," Tenzen told him. "Retrieving you from where you'd gone wasn't easy. You may see the world a little different from now on, too."

"You gave me... some of your powers? Shinigami powers?"

"Magic is magic, Rakurai. The only difference is that mine is nearly as old as this world. It changes the flavour."

"But gods are stronger, different."

"We can hold our powers without wearing out our bodies, that's all. When your ancestor reached the Otherworld on his spirit walk, the celestial magic he absorbed strengthened his body, so it could better withstand the ravages of time. He passed on this blessing to the clan he formed. To this day, the strongest Yuvine show their age the least. Have you never noticed that?"

"I've noticed that you are distracting me using my very own favourite technique." He smiled at the gorgeous man in whose lap he lay. "Did sharing my magic give you insights into my personality?"

"No. Holding your soul in my palm did that." Tenzen smiled suddenly, and Rakurai felt a weight lift from his mind. "I was delighted to discover that you appear to find me as attractive as I find you."

Rakurai knew he was blushing, but he didn't avert his eyes, nor did he object when Tenzen leaned down and very softly touched their lips together.

The air in the cave crackled as they made contact, and the sparks under Rakurai's skin answered. Heat flooded him, want grew and clamoured for attention, and Rakurai's last coherent thought was that he'd never thought to flavour kisses with lightning.

GROUND RULES

"Luring the rafeet will be ridiculously easy," Tenzen declared. He'd torn himself from Rakurai's embrace the moment he realised that he'd kissed the man to banish the cold, lonely sensation that had grown in his chest since he'd returned Rakurai's soul to his body.

Rakurai intrigued him. He'd made a bargain with the Unseen Power to save his life. While he'd persuaded Rakurai's soul back into his body, he'd admitted to himself that he wanted the Yuvine. But his desperation should not be their beginning.

He focused on what they wanted to achieve: free him from the rafeet's imprisonment and stop the creature's terror. One down. One to go.

He hurried out of the cave, heard Rakurai scramble to follow him, and wondered whether he had recovered sufficiently from his bout with death. Tenzen had drained the excess energy that had made Rakurai's skin tingle and his head buzz during their kiss, but his ministrations might have left other discomforts. And Rakurai, he'd learned, endured privations without complaint.

"Tenzen, wait! We're not done discussing this." Rakurai caught up with him, silver hair loose and dishevelled, lips red and a little swollen from their kisses. "Where are we going?"

"We need a lake to trap the rafeet. I remember a string of fishponds along the manor's western edge. I was going to explore them." He turned his head to study Rakurai. "You should stay here. You need more rest."

"I'm fine." Rakurai dismissed the concern. Then he narrowed his eyes. "You're entirely too confident. You're convinced that you can handle the rafeet all by yourself when before you told me we needed to fight it together. What are you planning? And why a lake?"

Tenzen resumed walking. "I could not wield lightning when I suggested we kill it together. Lightning makes it so much easier."

"Explain."

"The rafeet wants the souls I carry. It'll seek me out wherever I am. And being struck by lightning while standing in a lake will end the rafeet as surely as cutting out its heart."

"You wouldn't leave it with its heart, would you?"

"Of course not. But I can make my task easier and kill it first."

They walked in silence for a time. "How are you going to entice the rafeet into the water?"

"I'm going to find a lake with an island in the middle and hide the souls there."

Rakurai grabbed his arm and yanked him to a stop. "You suffered eighteen years of incarceration to keep the souls from the rafeet, and now you're going to use them as bait?"

"It won't get near them."

"You can't guarantee that. It already tricked you once. What if it has other weapons? Other wiles? If it takes the souls—"

"Rakurai—"

"No. This is insane. I know you're a death god, but those are the souls of humans and—"

Rakurai wasn't listening. He confronted a death god with blazing eyes and a conviction Tenzen felt like a physical touch. Rakurai believed in his duty, and Tenzen had never seen anything so enticing.

He didn't want to fight, so he did the next best thing. He pinned Rakurai to the nearest tree and kissed him.

This wasn't the soft, sensual kiss of earlier. This kiss was savage, with a touch of anger lacing the heat. Rakurai struggled, clawed at Tenzen's back, resisted the manhandling.

And then he went limp.

Tenzen eased his grip, not surprised when Rakurai evaded his hold with an eel-like move and planted him flat on his back two heartbeats later. He threw himself on top of Tenzen with a force that made them both grunt, and then it was his turn to take Tenzen's mouth.

The heat was still there, along with the savage need, but now there was no anger.

Tenzen wrapped his arms around Rakurai and grabbed huge handfuls of the silver hair to hold while Rakurai devoured his mouth.

"Don't try to persuade me with kisses," Rakurai said when he drew away. "It's not fair because I like kissing you. If we must fight, let's fight and kiss after."

"I wasn't attempting to persuade you with kisses. I was trying to make you listen."

"I realise that. Your frustration was plain. But my concerns are as valid as your frustration, Tenzen. How could you have guarded those souls for years, only to risk them now?"

Tenzen smoothed Rakurai's hair from his face. "The souls won't be at risk, because I'll be with them on that island. They'll never be out of my protection."

Rakurai blushed at the implied rebuke, and Tenzen had to fight not to pull him close and kiss him again. He had to remember that Rakurai wasn't aware of Tenzen's conviction that the two of them belonged together. Rakurai was not at the same point on their path. He might not be ready to die to save Tenzen's life.

Only… he'd already done so.

Tenzen froze.

"You look as if somebody hit you," Rakurai said, touching the back of his fingers to Tenzen's forehead. "Are you well?"

Tenzen scrambled for sense and sanity. He'd have settled for words, even. But this topic was too big to broach now. Or ever.

"We may need to find a different lake," he said, struggling to sitting while Rakurai crab-walked off his legs to let him stand. "You mentioned that the rafeet could have other weapons in its arsenal. What if it sends its spawn to swim across the lake and then uses them as a siphon to absorb the souls? We can kill them as they come, but in doing that, the rafeet will spot the trap."

Rakurai turned away, his muttered comment too low for Tenzen to hear.

He sprang to his feet and turned Rakurai to face him. "Say that again."

Rakurai kept his face averted. His ears were red. "The rafeet's spawn won't be a problem," Rakurai said, louder this time. "I... I checked on them while I was hunting for food. Free from the rafeet's control, they were mere husks without a will of their own. And since their souls were long gone..."

"Now who's being reckless? I was in no fit state to help you had you encountered the rafeet!"

"You were also in no fit state to help yourself had I done so. I'm aware that I put you in danger by leaving you alone. At the time I... didn't think beyond your need for food."

"Let's call it even, and this argument over. If the demonspawn are no longer a concern, then we'll find a fishpond to use as our trap. I'll be on the lake. You'll be on the bank. And as soon as the rafeet is in the water, we'll hit it with lightning."

He turned Rakurai towards him and lifted his chin with a finger. "Can I kiss you now to seal the deal?"

LIGHTNING STRIKES

The largest of the fishponds had a small island at its centre. Tenzen divested himself of the souls and settled beside them to wait. He hadn't been totally truthful with Rakurai. Guarding souls outside of his garden affected both his speed and his agility. When he carried as many souls as he'd collected in Shimabara, he'd have to set them aside to fight.

Not that it mattered. Without its spawn and the net between them, the rafeet would be like any other demon. And in his long life Tenzen had killed many.

He could have left the task to Rakurai, but aside from revenge for eighteen lost years, there was also the secret thrill of sharing a task with another.

He'd heard that three of his fellow death gods had bondmates, but he'd never wondered how that influenced their duties. Did they fight as a unit? Did they separate for the Shinigami to fulfil their tasks? He'd never bothered to find out, didn't even know what kind of mates they'd chosen.

No one but Tenzen had ever set foot inside Tenzen's garden. Now, he wanted to see Rakurai there.

Is anything amiss?

Rakurai's voice snapped him back to awareness. *What do you mean?*

All of a sudden you seemed miles away. As if I couldn't reach you even if I flew.

You can sense my location?

I don't know. I have... an awareness of you now.

Tenzen nodded, even though Rakurai couldn't see it. Not surprising, perhaps. *You gave me your magic and I shared my powers. I apologise if this distresses you.*

He felt Rakurai gather himself for an answer and waited with his heart beating absurdly fast.

Only for the rafeet to emerge from the trees with long, loping strides.

Undisguised, it was hideous. Tall and broad, with gnarly muscles and wrinkled skin that sagged in long, dry strips. Tiny piggish eyes and a huge maw filled with three rows of needle-pointed teeth created a face that belonged into a nightmare. Sensing the souls on the island, it laboured and slobbered, hunger and desire overriding caution and natural cunning.

Didn't you say the thing had fed recently? Tenzen asked. A well-fed, sated rafeet would be covered in smooth, supple skin. Not this barklike mess.

It ravaged the human world for at least a sennight. Maybe maintaining its spawn drains its power faster.

That's as good an explanation as any. I assume it sucked its spawn's souls dry of suffering a very long time ago. You said the spawn you killed were soulless dead.

They turned to dust when I touched them, Rakurai replied, and Tenzen heard the revulsion in this tone. Soulless creatures were abominations that scared even a death god. No wonder they bothered a Yuvine.

The rafeet sniffed along the bank, searching for a way to the island. Rakurai moved with it, keeping out of sight and a clear section of lake between them.

Tenzen tracked the gleam of Rakurai's hair with half his attention, keeping the rest on the rafeet. He'd never used lightning, and his fingertips tingled with the unfamiliar power. Impatient, Tenzen lifted the shield he'd placed over the souls by a fraction and let a hint of their essence waft across the lake.

The rafeet howled and threw himself into the water. It splashed and paddled towards the island, uncoordinated, but at a speed that caught Tenzen by surprise. He fumbled for the lightning when Rakurai's glowing whip skimmed the lake's surface and hit the rafeet in the head.

Its scream raised every hair on Tenzen's body.

The rafeet thrashed, creating a wave that washed around the lake. When it scrambled to reach the safety of the shore, Tenzen was ready with his own lightning whip, hitting the rafeet in the chest as it reared up.

Rakurai stood ready on the bank. Lightning shot from both his hands, one bolt hitting the rafeet, the others charging the water until black, oily smoke obscured the roiling surface.

The rafeet floated on its back, ravaged face lifted to the sky. Tenzen sent the body to the edge of the lake, where Rakurai waited, soul sword in hand. He opened the demon's chest with one long stroke, removed the heart, and set it on a nearby rock where he lashed it with lightning until all that was left of the rafeet was a scorch mark.

Tenzen gathered the souls before the stink of burning flesh, old leather, and grave rot could reach and distress them. Then he waited, hands outstretched and open, until the rafeet's soul settled in his palm. The touch bit like acid and tasted of old hurts, but Tenzen didn't flinch. Not every soul he gathered was ready for its next life. If souls moved on that easily, he wouldn't need his garden.

He added the rafeet's soul to the others in his keeping and then joined Rakurai by the lakeshore.

Sweat dewed along Rakurai's hairline. He had his hands braced on his knees and breathed as if he'd been running.

Tenzen wrapped an arm around his shoulders. *You were not strong enough yet to use your lightning*, he chided gently, mind-to-mind to soften the rebuke. *I want you to come with me. Spend time in my garden. Heal and recover.*

Rakurai didn't answer. He stared at the scorched rock, his eyes dull and lifeless. Rakurai was a hunter but ending a life—even that of a demon who thrived on pain and suffering—brought him no pleasure.

The image of Rakurai in Tenzen's garden became a want that was hard to shake. This time, Tenzen didn't ask. He opened the veil and pulled Rakurai with him as he stepped through.

Soul Garden

Summer-warm air brushed Rakurai's face as he set foot in Tenzen's garden. The sky stretched deep blue overhead, and a soft breeze blew a myriad of scents towards him. After the red and gold autumn hues around the rafeet's manor, Rakurai struggled to adapt to the mass of colour in this cheerful jungle, where trees, shrubs, and flowers grew as they pleased and where butterflies tumbled from petal to petal without a care— hundreds, maybe thousands of them, in colours and sizes Rakurai had never seen before.

Enchanted by the spectacle, Rakurai hadn't noticed Tenzen leaving his side. Not until the Shinigami returned, an indulgent smile on his face. "It's a joy to see them here after all this time."

"These are the souls you've guarded?"

"Some of them. The others were already in my care." He laced his fingers with Rakurai's and tugged him along a narrow path. "Let them recover and find their way around the garden."

Tenzen moved deftly between bushes and giant ferns, not minding that fronds and branches tugged on his clothes and hair.

Between the wonders of the garden and the enchanting view of a relaxed Tenzen, Rakurai had much to take in. He pulled Tenzen to a stop as the path opened into a small meadow. "Who maintains all this when you're not here?"

"Soul gardens adapt to the needs of the souls residing here. It's… difficult to explain. The garden doesn't exist in either of the worlds. It's remade whenever a soul needs shelter."

"If there were no souls here, there would be no garden?"

"Correct. Though it's not a fate I'd like to think about. That'd be…"

"The end of the worlds?"

"Yes. Souls have passed through the veil long before your ancestor reached the Otherworld. I don't want to imagine a time when they might not do so. It will come to pass, I know that. But I've tended my garden since the beginning of time, and I'd like to think that the end is millennia in the future."

They stood in silence while Rakurai digested that. Humans might live eighty years. He was centuries older and—by Yuvine standards—still a young man. The Shinigami were immortal. "I can't imagine all the years you've lived," he whispered, awed and humbled. "All you've seen. The people you've met." *The time you've spent alone.*

The kisses they'd shared seemed insignificant by comparison.

"Is it always summer in your garden?" he asked to distract himself.

"No. I told you the garden adapts to the souls sheltering here. What kind of garden it becomes is as much a surprise to me as it is to you."

"You don't know how your garden will appear?"

"No. Walk with me, and you'll see. It can be—and at times has been—a Zen garden, austere and serene with its shapes representing other concepts. It can become a forest covered in snow. Or a riot of colour as it is now. When many souls reside here, it's a garden composed of smaller gardens." He smiled a little. "It was a rose garden once. Nothing but roses as far as you could walk. I spent days here, just enjoying the fragrance."

Rakurai followed Tenzen across the meadow. He trailed the fingers of his free hand through the tops of the tall grasses and inhaled the scents of wildflowers until the meadow became an orchard and they stopped again to gaze. "This isn't the garden I would build, but I'm enjoying this."

"The fact that you would *build* a garden tells me a lot about you." Tenzen slipped his arms around Rakurai's middle and pulled them flush together, leaving Rakurai with no doubt of his interest. "I'm thinking austere and serene would describe it well, no?"

Rakurai let his weight rest against Tenzen. "I like rocks. And order."

"Then come this way. I've one more task to complete here before I may rest."

The garden changed as they walked, the riotous tumble of plants giving way to a more structured design of large-headed dahlias planted in rows of differing colours. In another corner, flowers that never shared a season bloomed side by side as if nature had decided it didn't matter. And while the sight of a cherry tree laden with blossom beside a tree weighed down with ripe apples confused a part of Rakurai's mind, he also delighted in the unexpected sight.

"My garden provides exactly the nourishment each soul needs to prepare for its onward journey," Tenzen explained from beside him.

"What happens to beings that don't have souls? Or to souls that don't deserve an onward journey?"

Tenzen pointed to a far corner of the garden that was arid and bare, not in the contemplative sparseness of a Zen garden, but with jagged rocks and sharp-spiked plants. A sense of desolation wafted towards them as they came near.

"All souls deserve an onward journey," he said and held out his hand. A small butterfly appeared in his palm, wings ragged and of no discernible colour. It seemed timid, unsure whether to leave the shelter of

Tenzen's palm. But Tenzen stood unmoving with his hand held out, patient as the end of the world, until the butterfly took flight. "All souls deserve an onward journey," he repeated. "Some don't know themselves well enough to understand their own needs. Those souls spend more time here until they've gained the wisdom they need for their next life."

"This is not what the Yuvine would call an appropriate punishment for sinners."

"You can't know that. You're not a soul confined to my garden. Just because you would enjoy it here, does not mean that everyone else feels the same. Besides, confinement to my garden doesn't mean what you seem to think it does." He wrapped his arms around Rakurai's waist once more and nestled his cheek against Rakurai's. "Enough of my business now," he murmured. "We have a completed mission to celebrate. And I very much enjoyed kissing you and would like to do more of it."

A shiver washed through Rakurai, intensifying when Tenzen nuzzled his neck.

"In fact, I want to love you for hours and days."

Rakurai's chuckle held a tinge of nerves, but he let Tenzen hold him. "I'm not opposed to the idea. We never made use of the hot spring in the back of the cave, and I could do with washing all this dust off me." Another shiver flashed across his skin as he pictured a wet, naked Tenzen, stretched out in hot, steaming water.

Tenzen tightened his arms. "Well, if it's hot water you have a hankering for…"

FOOD AND COMPANY

A square of carefully raked gravel stretched along the wall enclosing Tenzen's home. Mossy rocks lay in heaps as if tumbled there by a torrent of water. And close to where the last rock had landed was a bathing area.

Rough steppingstones, alternating with stretches of smooth wooden decking, led to an enclosed soaking pond. Steam rose from its surface in thin whirls, and the feed bringing the hot water was hidden under more heaps of stone. Paper lanterns hung from the rafters of the slatted cover sheltering the bathing space, and stone lanterns lined the edge of the decking and dotted the rockfalls in strategic places. It wasn't dark yet, but Tenzen knew how the space appeared when the light faded and the sun went down, and he looked forward to sharing the peace with Rakurai.

"Might this be more your style of garden?" It wasn't a difficult guess, judging by Rakurai's awestruck face.

"It's magnificent," Rakurai whispered. "And makes me more aware of how filthy I am."

"Go ahead and bathe." Tenzen pointed to the area off to one side, where a stool and bucket waited next to a dish of soap.

He lifted the wards and glamours that preserved his home when he was away and entered through the shoji at the back, intending to find yukata for Rakurai and himself, as well as a few delicacies they could share while they soaked. It would be no hardship to summon those items, but after his long imprisonment he enjoyed the normalcy of walking, even if it was just from his veranda to his sleeping chamber and back.

Rakurai had stripped off his filthy clothes by the time Tenzen returned and he stood, gloriously nude, one foot on the stool as he soaped his body. His shoulders were broad, his arms and chest well-muscled. Long, strong legs led to a trim waist, and his backside—round and firm—was a magnet that drew Tenzen's gaze and made his fingers itch to touch.

Tenzen set down the yukata—deep blue for Rakurai, white for himself—and placed his tray on the edge of the soaking tub. It held bite-sized treats he'd fantasised about while the rafeet had held him trapped: rice balls filled with roast pork, steamed fish in a delicate, sweet-salty glaze, crisp tofu in broth, and tiny seaweed parcels filled with braised roots and mushrooms.

It was simple fare to enjoy while sharing the bath. Tenzen hoped that the dishes would be to Rakurai's liking. He would ask later what the Yuvine enjoyed most and provide it for dinner. For now, he would wash eighteen years of captivity off his skin and relish the sight of Rakurai and his company in a place where no one but him had ever set foot before.

"You're looking at me," Rakurai said without turning around.

"You're worth looking at," Tenzen replied. "I like seeing you in my home, as much as I enjoyed seeing you in my garden."

Rakurai's silver hair and pale skin made the blush exceptionally noticeable. Tenzen felt warm, imagining the two of them twined together. He pictured the silver tresses spread across his pillows, conjured the sight of finger bruises on the pale skin. And he craved the one thing that he couldn't quite imagine: The sight of Rakurai in the throes of bliss.

Tenzen reached for the bucket. He scooped up a measure of hot water and stepped behind Rakurai, ready to help him rinse the suds from his skin. Rakurai did not flinch away. He tilted his head and let Tenzen douse him with clean water, not hiding that his breath came faster at the attention. The long line of Rakurai's throat drew Tenzen's gaze, as did Rakurai's cock, attempting to curl towards his stomach. Tenzen wanted to touch, and caress, and possess all at once. He held himself back, replenished the water and finished rinsing Rakurai's hair. "Go, soak."

Rakurai tossed his wet tresses over one shoulder. "You don't want help washing?"

The suggestive timbre of his voice did little for Tenzen's peace of mind. "If you put your hands on me, we'll never make it into the tub. And I do want a soak."

"Is that so?" Rakurai trailed two fingers from the hollow at Tenzen's throat over his dishevelled, dirty robes down to his navel. The touch was light, but Tenzen felt it as if Rakurai used a branding iron. It sizzled along his nerves, leaving his skin feeling hot and cold all at once. "I'll go and soak, then. But know, Tenzen, that I will not take my eyes off you."

Rakurai's stomach rumbled a loud complaint, and they both stared at one another in surprise before they burst out laughing.

"Go, soak," Tenzen said again, as the haze of want thinned a smidgen. "There's food, too. Enough to hold us until dinner."

"A thoughtful host. You have my gratitude."

Rakurai settled in the soaking tub and Tenzen shed his clothes, not caring where they landed.

The soap smelled of cedar and spices and while he was keen to join Rakurai, he took his time lathering and scrubbing until he could no longer smell the rafeet's poison on his skin.

When he settled into the hot water he closed his eyes, relieved to be home and excited to have a gorgeous man by his side. The ends of his hair floated in the water and mingled with Rakurai's silver strands. Tenzen felt the touch and tangle and pictured it in his mind, too content to open his eyes.

They relaxed in the bath as the air around them cooled, the sun sank behind the trees, and the shadows grew longer. They shared the food and Tenzen added bottles of sake to the tray and refilled the dishes with whatever they had a hankering for. He hadn't planned to spend the afternoon with Rakurai in a soaking tub, but he saw little reason to leave.

Night, when it came, came swiftly, and Tenzen lit the lamps in the garden with a thought.

"That's a handy skill," Rakurai approved. "If I tried this at home, I'd be disturbing the gravel."

Tenzen chuckled and wound a strand of Rakurai's hair around his fingers. "Disturbing the order of your garden is unacceptable?"

"It is. Even for lights. I've placed my lanterns so they can be reached from beyond the raked gravel, but the positions are not ideal."

"You could use steppingstones."

"They'd destroy the symmetry I've aimed to achieve." He blushed, just before his smile grew wide and delighted, as if he'd had a revelation. "I need to redesign my garden. I have clearly made an unwise compromise."

"We all make compromises," Tenzen said quietly.

But Rakurai's impish mood from earlier in the day had returned and he didn't follow the line of conversation Tenzen was starting. "Do you feel that we are procrastinating over what we know is coming?"

"Is that so bad a thing?"

"Not at all. We deserved the rest. But we are both familiar with the steps of this dance, even if we've not danced it in a while. Correct?" A delicate pink blush stained his cheekbones, but he didn't look away and he didn't lose his smile. "I was bonded for two hundred years," he said with candour. "I've not lain with a man since long before that."

"You haven't wanted to?"

"Not since I was young. Naomi and I were friends. We chose to be bonded because... well... the Yuvine aren't numerous, and we both thought we could raise a child."

"And before you were bonded?"

"I had a few lovers. They usually complained that I didn't make enough time for them." He shrugged, as if he'd long reconciled himself to that before he slanted a look at Tenzen, sideways through his lashes. "I don't think I come highly recommended in that regard. What about you?"

"I like my solitude," Tenzen said. "There are death gods who've taken a mate and spoken bonding vows. I don't know how that works for them."

"But you've had lovers."

"I had bed partners. I spent a few pleasurable hours with someone I met and took a fancy to. That's all. I've never brought anyone to this house. Or to my garden."

"You said that earlier."

"Because you… you fit. I find that the most wondrous gift of all."

Rakurai rose from the water with a splash and held out his hand. "Let's see if we can improve on that."

CONNECTING

The white yukata brought out the lustre of Tenzen's dark hair. Rakurai wanted to bury his hands in the long strands almost as much as he wanted to strip the white cloth from Tenzen's shoulders. Arousal simmered in his blood and spread like an itch under his skin. Judging by the heat in his gaze, Tenzen felt the same. But despite having spent hours side by side, they'd yet to kiss again.

Despite his lack of practice, Rakurai enjoyed the mix of advance and retreat, of anticipation and reluctance. When Tenzen held out his hand, Rakurai took it without hesitation and followed him into the house.

Smooth wood, cool and solid under his bare feet, alternated with the slick springiness of the tatami matting. Lamplight spread a yellow glow until Tenzen slid the screen at the end of the hallway aside and pulled Rakurai into his bedchamber.

No lamps burned here, but the room wasn't dark. Silvery moonlight flooded through the open screens, along with the sounds and scents of the garden at night.

"I could be standing in my own chamber." Rakurai contemplated the play of the moonlight on rock and gravel. "I never saw the Otherworld as somewhere I wanted to spend more time, but this place, your home, has a peace and beauty all its own."

"It matches yours."

Rakurai swallowed a nervous chuckle. "I've never considered myself beautiful."

"You should. Your colouring is like the play of light and shadow and pleasing to my eyes."

Rakurai turned until his view included both Tenzen and the formal garden. "As is yours," he said, feasting his eyes on the man he was going to share a sleeping mat with. Tenzen stood in the centre of the room, tall and straight, swathed in shadows and mystery despite the white robe. "And I can't help but wonder what you'd look like in my home. In my garden."

He crossed the room and cupped Tenzen's face before touching their lips together in a chaste kiss. "I thought Shinigami were stern and chilly creatures who judged the lives of mortals. But you're kinder than most mortals I've ever met."

Tenzen clasped his hip and pulled him closer and Rakurai looped his arms around Tenzen's neck, so their breaths mingled as they spoke.

"I do judge the souls of mortals. And I can be," a corner of Tenzen's mouth quirked up, "what did you call it? 'Stern and chilly'. But I judge mortals by their actions. And yours have earned you nothing but kindness and my gratitude."

Rakurai's face heated and his heart picked up its pace. He hadn't acted from kindness when he'd found the Shinigami trapped on a plinth. He'd just followed the demands of his honour. To earn praise for doing his duty seemed wrong.

"And want has nothing to do with it?" He nuzzled into the soft space beneath Tenzen's ear and was rewarded with a shiver and a tightening of Tenzen's grip.

"Want and attraction might have had us sharing pleasure in the cave," he said, parting Rakurai's yukata with a fingertip. "Bringing you to my garden and my home…"

He smiled that devastating smile that had captivated Rakurai the first time he'd seen it, and when he touched Rakurai's chest, it was Rakurai's turn to shiver.

They'd taken their time, had enjoyed each other's company while letting the desire build. Now Rakurai felt as if he stood on a cliff, staring into a roiling sea that lay many fathoms beneath him. His nerves were strung taut, and anticipation swirled in his gut. Yet he was desperate to jump. He didn't recall this hunger, this rush of wanting from any of his previous affairs. And judging by the way blackness bled into Tenzen's violet eyes, he was not the only one affected.

"Touch me," he begged. "Put your hands on me and kiss me."

He met Tenzen's lips with a groan, felt his yukata shift open and reached for Tenzen's belt. He shoved the fabric aside until skin touched hot skin, his arms around Tenzen's waist and Tenzen's hands in his hair.

Tenzen kissed him as if he were starving and Rakurai gave himself up to that demanding mouth and the heat spiralling through him. His body tightened when Tenzen flicked one of his nipples, tightened more at the rhythmic grip and relaxation of Tenzen's hand on his hip. And when Tenzen left this mouth and sucked the lobe of his ear between his lips, Rakurai arched and almost came.

A sharp nip kicked the impending orgasm back a step. But it left Rakurai shaking, with blurry vision and almost unable to speak.

Oh kami! He didn't even want to imagine what would happen when he and Tenzen were joined. No doubt they'd set the house on fire.

He found a distraction in Tenzen's hair and skin, trailed kisses over Tenzen's neck and nuzzled the hollow of his throat, paying attention to every tiny groan and indrawn breath. Small nips and bites produced pleasure-filled gasps, his tongue on Tenzen's skin drew soft groans, and roaming touches turned Tenzen's breathing as ragged as Rakurai's.

Until Tenzen's grip imprisoned his hands. "I want all of you."

The heat in Tenzen's eyes took every sane thought from Rakurai's mind. Words failed him, but he tilted his head and offered his throat in invitation. And when Tenzen guided them deeper into the room and down onto the thick futon, he went eagerly.

The linens cooled his flushed skin. Scents of cedar and spice mingled with the musk of their desire. He ran his hands over Tenzen's flanks and the swell of his arse, relished the weight pressing him into the bed. He'd long forgotten the feel of another man's body twined with his. Tenzen's hot mouth, the mix of hard muscles and smooth planes, and the tight clutch of his hands were an excellent reminder.

"Now, Tenzen. Please," he begged when he could not bear any more delay to their joining. They were both flushed, sweaty, panting and so on edge that Rakurai had no idea how they were still holding back. He ached with want, and Tenzen's rigid length and the fire in his near-black gaze promised him release. "Tenzen!"

The Shinigami finally relented. He reached for the oil and slicked himself. Then, kneeling, he slung Rakurai's legs over his shoulders, and slowly, far more slowly than Rakurai thought possible, pushed into Rakurai.

"Oh kami!" Rakurai breathed through the stretch and burn. "More!" He melted into the sheets as he relaxed his muscles, giving way to Tenzen.

"You're... so... tight." Tenzen rocked, holding himself rigid, but driving deeper on each exhale. "So... damned... tight."

And then, with one hard thrust, he slid home.

"Fuck!" Rakurai drew out the word, revelling in the feeling of heat and fullness. "Kiss me."

Tenzen curled forward and took his mouth, deep and hard, his tongue mimicking the thrusts of his hips. Rakurai was bent almost in half, and he didn't care. He wanted Tenzen's mouth, his cock, the fingers clenching on his hips hard enough to bruise.

He wanted everything. And more.

Their bodies slapped together, hard and insistent. A touch very like lightning flashed along his spine. Every time Tenzen pushed home it sparked brighter, higher and hotter, until his toes curled. His muscles drew tight, his back bowed, and then he screamed out his release into the stillness of the night and Tenzen joined him moments later.

"We need another bath," Tenzen murmured before Rakurai's breathing could slow and deepen towards sleep. "And food."

"Later," Rakurai mumbled.

"How much later?" Tenzen ran his palm over Rakurai's arse. He'd not had nearly enough of Rakurai's intoxicating mix of fierce and yielding. "Before or after you scream my name?"

A shiver ran over Rakurai's skin, and he opened his eyes. They weren't sleepy at all.

He traced his fingers over Tenzen's chest and left tingles in their wake. And when he took hold of Tenzen's cock, it was Tenzen who had to swallow a scream.

Rakurai stroked the silky skin, his touch like fire and ice, before he closed his fingers around Tenzen's shaft and jerked him in long, smooth movements. Each stroke zinged through Tenzen from head to foot, leaving him shivering and weak.

"Wha—"

Rakurai didn't answer. He leaned in for a kiss while his hand continued to move.

Tenzen wrapped both arms around him, desperate to keep him close.

"Don't stop," he begged, as fire rushed through him in ways he'd never felt before. "Don't even think—"

Rakurai tightened his grip. He kissed along Tenzen's jaw, then followed the line of Tenzen's neck to the hollow of this throat.

A gentle bite had Tenzen almost arch off the bed, and Rakurai hummed his approval and did it again.

Light turned to dark, and cold to hot. Tenzen's body hummed. He scrabbled for purchase on sweaty skin while he was caught between the touches of Rakurai's hand and mouth.

Rakurai's deep, raspy chuckle brought Tenzen another step closer to bliss. Sparkles danced along the edges of his vision, his release close enough to touch while at the same time still so far away.

"Rakurai, please! Now!" Tenzen pushed into Rakurai's fist, begging with his whole body for the icy hot touch until Rakurai sped his strokes and the ozone bite in the air revealed his mastery of lightning.

"I didn't think you'd have this many scars," Tenzen murmured later. They'd bathed and enjoyed a late meal before returning to Tenzen's futon. Fed and mellow, Tenzen was content to run his palms up Rakurai's arms and down his chest as if he were stroking a kitten.

Rakurai stretched under his touch. "Not all Yuvine neglect their duties."

"Clearly not." His fingers stopped at a fresh mark in the centre of Rakurai's chest. "This is recent."

"It's nothing. Ambush on the road."

Tenzen saw the scene as Rakurai spoke of it, saw the four attackers who'd died, and the one who'd fled. "You thought they were there for you."

The lazy contentment was gone from Rakurai's voice as he spoke. "I have no proof. But Yamakage Daisuke, the head of my clan, cossets that secretary of his. I can't imagine the man has to turn to robbery to meet his needs."

"Why would he want to attack you?"

"Daisuke's not exactly fond of me, and right now less than ever. For one, I don't blindly follow orders—"

Tenzen laughed. "I wouldn't have guessed."

"Right. For another, I abide by the rules laid down by Yamakage Jumon."

"And your clan elder does not?"

"Many of the Yuvine elders now *interpret* the rules that don't suit them, saying Jumon couldn't have foreseen their needs," Rakurai explained. "They've started to meddle in human politics, claiming they're only protecting the interests of the Yuvine. But that's not the worst. The Yuvine are not numerous. To kill two of our own on the say-so of an elder…"

"Is that what he ordered you to do?"

"Yes."

"And you refused."

"I refused. Daisuke thinks it's not my place to question his orders. And he holds grudges. So… he may have wanted to punish me." He smiled suddenly. "He knows how much Raijin means to me. How I try to spend as much time with him as I can. Sending me on this demon hunt was punishment, I'm sure. He couldn't have dreamed that I'd meet you."

"Or that I'd be so taken with you that we're—"

A deep flush painted Rakurai's cheeks. "Definitely not. I think he's never looked at another man that way."

"Not even his secretary?"

"I doubt it. Flattery is the way to win his heart, not passion."

"How about *your* heart?" Tenzen murmured. He tweaked a dusky nipple and watched Rakurai's eyes flutter shut. "Can that be won by passion?"

"Why don't you find out?"

Tenzen rolled until he had Rakurai under him, his weight pressing him into the bed. "I'm intending to do just that."

Reasons for Leaving

Rakurai woke to thin, watery light streaming through the open shoji screen. Floating clouds painted patterns on the tatami, and the chilly morning air carried the scents of pine and resin.

He stretched, feeling rested despite the early hour, and tried to remember how many days he'd been Tenzen's guest. They fit together so seamlessly, in bed and out, that he'd barely noticed the time passing.

They walked through the gardens and trained in the dojo that occupied a whole wing of the house. They had tea in the sunshine, shared the hot tub, and made love whenever and wherever the mood took them.

Rakurai could imagine spending all his years in Tenzen's home without experiencing a moment of boredom or a wish to be elsewhere. He'd never felt so carefree. Nor had he ever talked so much.

Tenzen's knowledge was vast, his experiences far outstripping Rakurai's. Despite that, he never stopped asking questions: about Rakurai's life, about the human world, about the Yuvine.

Rakurai answered every one and asked plenty of his own in return.

He rolled off the futon and stepped onto the veranda, surprised to find himself alone. On every other morning, he'd found Tenzen drinking tea in the sun, still wearing his white yukata and with his hair flowing loose around his shoulders. Now the veranda lay empty, and neither checking left where Tenzen's dojo bordered the garden, nor right along the walkway that led to the bathing area, produced a sign of the Shinigami.

Rakurai returned to the bedroom to dress, wondering what had become of his lover.

Death gods had their duties, but not knowing where Tenzen had gone disturbed Rakurai's balance. Tenzen was a solitary man. He was lonely, too, and didn't deserve such a fate. In only a few days, Rakurai's attraction had blossomed from wanting into warmth. And simple kindness had grown into concern that even a vigorous workout in Tenzen's beautiful dojo couldn't ease completely.

He was in Tenzen's house without Tenzen, and as the day wore on, Rakurai finally admitted that he missed him.

He'd arrived at that revelation when the veil opened and Tenzen stepped through. His white robe was free of stains and wrinkles, but Rakurai, with a gaze sharpened by worry, saw through the glamour.

Tenzen's long hair was braided for battle. His fingerless leather gloves were as scuffed and muddy as his boots. And when he took three steps towards Rakurai, he favoured his left side.

Rakurai was up and across the room in an instant, scanning every inch of Tenzen's form. He slipped under Tenzen's right arm, offering support. Tenzen leaned against him, warm and heavy, and Rakurai released the breath he'd been holding.

"How badly are you hurt?"

"Just in need of rest." The halting steps and tiny lines of pain around Tenzen's mouth gave the lie to his words. They also suggested that he'd fought beyond his reserves.

Rakurai had the perfect remedy for Tenzen's exhaustion.

Days of sharing pleasure had taught him more control over his lightning than he'd learnt in the six hundred years since his birth. Holding Tenzen upright with an arm around his waist, he raised his left hand and sent a tiny lightning bolt sizzling into Tenzen's chest.

Tenzen rocked in Rakurai's hold. He exhaled in a short huff, but he didn't stop leaning, so Rakurai sent another bolt and another. Compared to the lightning that had restored Tenzen's health after his captivity, these charges didn't tax Rakurai's strength, and Tenzen absorbed each one with a small exhalation until he straightened, standing on his own.

"Watching you do this is arousing beyond words. I've never seen anyone wield lightning before." He leaned to kiss Rakurai's mouth. "Thank you."

"No need. You'd do the same for me."

"If I had the control. If I attempted it now, I'd kill you."

That was true. Tenzen could fell a tree using his new ability. He couldn't light a candle.

"You'll learn it soon enough."

"Yes, I will." He took a few steps across the room, moving more easily with his back and shoulders straight. "A long soak will finish restoring me."

Rakurai didn't argue. He followed Tenzen to the bathing area, helped him strip and wash down.

A myriad of healing cuts marred Tenzen's skin along with deeper wounds where claws had slashed his side.

"If this is your definition of not much damage…" Rakurai brushed the deepest of the cuts, not surprised that Tenzen hadn't been able to hide all the effects of the fight. "Shouldn't you have spent more time healing in your garden?"

"Possibly. But I hadn't left word for your where I'd gone and, besides…" He quirked a tiny smile. "I missed you."

Rakurai wanted to be annoyed, but the warmth blooming in his chest made that next to impossible. "I'll feed you more lightning later," he said as he helped Tenzen into the tub.

"I'd appreciate it." Tenzen settled deep into the water and rested his head against the padded edge of the tub. A tray of food materialised on the rim. Rakurai perched beside it and took pleasure in feeding Tenzen his favourite rice balls and dumplings. He wanted to know where Tenzen had been, but he held his peace until the dishes were empty.

"What happened?"

"Demons attacked my garden. They were uncommonly organised and already in formation when I arrived. It was an uphill battle."

"Why didn't you call for me?"

Tenzen kept his eyes closed and his face averted.

Rakurai's temper spiked. "Do you think me so lacking?"

That brought Tenzen's head around. When his eyes opened, they held an emotion Rakurai couldn't identify. "I didn't think you were lacking. I just…"

Rakurai waited until he was sure Tenzen would say nothing further. "You just what, Tenzen? You've complained that there are never any Yuvine nearby when there are demon attacks. I was right here. All it needed was a moment's warning to let me arm myself."

Tenzen's cheeks were pink, and Rakurai didn't think the flush came from the heat of the water.

"I've always fought alone. I thought to ask your help, but…"

"I will always answer your call," Rakurai said, settling his palm over the fading wound in Tenzen's side. "I want your word that you won't hesitate to reach out to me."

Tenzen held Rakurai's gaze. "I promise. Now join me in the tub."

"I've been feeling restless all day," Rakurai admitted later as they sat beside the open screen in Tenzen's bedroom sharing tea. "It's the first time I've thought of returning home, not because I want to leave you, but—"

"You're a Yuvine. And it is nearing mid-winter. Of course you'd be restless."

Rakurai's jaw dropped. "Mid-winter? How... What...?" His mind sputtered through questions that made no sense. They'd been a week away from the autumn equinox when Elder Daisuke had sent him after the rafeet. He'd spent three days on the road, then... four days? Five...? Working to free Tenzen and kill the demon. And then— "I haven't been here for two whole months!"

"I may have... blurred the passage of time a little."

In all their conversations, Rakurai had never asked about the extent of Tenzen's powers. Now he remembered his teachers' warnings: *Don't trust a death god. Don't accept any boon they offer. And never do their bidding.*

He'd trusted Tenzen.

And Tenzen had stopped him from realising how much time was passing.

Anger and a hefty dose of guilt made him rise and put distance between himself and his Shinigami lover.

"I have a son, Tenzen. You know that. I also told you that my clan elders are not exactly pleased with me. Did it ever occur to you that Raijin might be in danger without me there to look out for him?"

"He wasn't without a guardian," Tenzen said softly. "I've watched over him since the moment you told me of his existence."

Rakurai didn't want to listen to excuses. He paced the wooden boards with long, angry strides and kept his gaze on his feet. It wasn't behaviour suited to a seasoned hunter, but he didn't want to say anything he'd regret later.

His duties often took him away from home and he had little control over the length of his absences. This time had been different. Once the rafeet was dead, he'd chosen to visit with Tenzen, had decided to take a few days just for himself.

Only for these few days to turn into weeks without him being aware of it.

"Did you interfere with my thoughts? My memories?"

"No."

"How can I believe you?"

"Watch." Tenzen waved his hand and the air shimmered like light blooming behind a gauze curtain. The shadowy image grew clearer and Rakurai saw his home and Raijin bent over a writing desk. Judging from the books surrounding him, he worked on a translation, but Rakurai couldn't tell which of the many scrolls from his library had caught Raijin's attention.

"Can he hear me? See me?"

"No. And no. This is how I keep an eye on events in the human realm. I need to open the veil to interact. But I have watched over him, Rakurai. I would have alerted you immediately had there been need."

"But why Tenzen? Why hide the passage of time from me? Raijin spent all this time alone in the house with just his tutors. I've missed weeks of conversation with him." Guilt gnawed at him when he considered how he'd spent this time.

"I should have warned you. Let you return home sooner. Only I found that I... enjoy having a companion more than I thought."

The softly spoken words stopped Rakurai's tirade before it could start. He was no stranger to loneliness, and he'd struggled to imagine what Tenzen's life had been like. Always alone with nothing but his duty to fill his days.

"I enjoy spending time with you, too." He stood irresolute in the centre of the room, his gaze skittering from Tenzen to the image of his son above the quiet garden, and back to Tenzen.

"I know you want leave, and I won't stop you," Tenzen said, very quietly. "But I will miss you."

Rakurai returned to his cushion. He set the teapot into the brazier to re-heat the tea before he refilled their cups. "I'm a Yuvine hunter, Tenzen. Sworn to defend the human realm. I must return to my home and my work. But I'd hoped that we could continue to meet," he said, not taking his eyes from Tenzen. "I've already offered to fight beside you should you need my help. I promised, Tenzen, and as a Yuvine the Otherworld is not barred to me."

Tenzen's expression brightened. He didn't ask whether Rakurai was serious. He just held out his hand.

When Rakurai mirrored the gesture, he closed his fingers around Rakurai's and held on tight.

NOT A GOODBYE

Their lovemaking that night was fierce and tender and left a bittersweet taste in Tenzen's mouth. He lay awake after Rakurai had fallen asleep, determined not to lose one moment of his presence. He watched moonbeams wander through the room and grey light announce the arrival of morning, wishing that the veil did not exist. That he could pass from world to world as easily as Rakurai.

That singular gift was wasted on the Yuvine. Once, they'd been a common sight in the Otherworld. Now, few travelled between the worlds. Most were content to reside in the human realm where their gifts seemed like magic and humans bowed to them.

Tenzen pushed the thought aside and returned to studying Rakurai's face. His lover followed the rules set down by Yamakage Jumon. He moved between the worlds and fought to hold back the darkness. Rakurai's magic was as strong as his spirit. He would live for centuries more and Tenzen did not want to spoil the time they had together by dwelling on what he couldn't change.

Rakurai's silver hair glimmered in the darkness of the bedroom. Tenzen held a handful of it to the moonlight, the way he'd done in those interminable hours while he'd pleaded with Rakurai's soul to return to his body.

Then as now, the act brought memories.

Only once before had Tenzen tried to coax a soul from the path it had chosen. That time, he'd failed. Yamakage Jumon had decided that he'd lived long enough, and nothing Tenzen had said had persuaded him otherwise.

While he'd argued with Rakurai's soul, Tenzen had feared that the younger Yamakage would be as stubborn as the older one.

"You're not sleeping?"

Fatigue blurred Rakurai's voice. Tenzen pulled him closer and let his fingertips trail up and down Rakurai's back. "I need less sleep than you do. And I'm comfortable where I am."

Rakurai sighed and his limbs grew heavy once more. He wouldn't remember this exchange come morning since he'd never really woken. And Tenzen would miss his company, but he wouldn't fight Rakurai over his need to return to his son.

They would keep talking to each other.

They would meet.

And when the need arose, they would fight back-to-back.

Tenzen was sure the turmoil in his mind would rob him of all sleep, but Rakurai's warmth tempered the chill in his soul, and when he blinked himself back to awareness, a rosy tinge coloured the sky and Rakurai was awake beside him.

They kissed, slowly and carefully, while Tenzen's mind recorded details: the taste of Rakurai's lips, the exact curve of his elegant spine, the angles and planes of back and chest, the silkiness of his skin and texture of his hair.

When Rakurai drew away he looked well-kissed, but his eyes held neither the heat nor the delighted sparkle Tenzen had grown accustomed to seeing.

"I must check on Raijin," Rakurai said when the eastern sky bloomed with the colours of sunrise. "As much as I wish to stay here, I can't be selfish and deprive Raijin of his father. I don't want him growing up guided by the clan elders. He doesn't deserve that."

"But you will visit."

"Yes. I swear. I'll visit whenever I can. And once Raijin is grown…."

Tenzen pulled him close and buried his face in Rakurai's hair. "Then nothing more needs to be said."

Tenzen had never considered how many things one could do for the last time in one morning. Share a bath, pour tea, breakfast while sitting on the veranda watching the sun wake the world. All were common tasks he'd performed countless times since meeting Rakurai. Yet suddenly, each one brought a lump to his throat or an uncomfortable churning to his gut.

Tenzen ignored them as best he could and focused on Rakurai.

His lover hadn't eaten. He cradled his teacup as if he needed the warmth, while his gaze roamed the garden, not settling on any one thing, and tension drew his shoulders into a taut line.

"What worries you?"

Rakurai blew out a breath. "You. You worry me, Tenzen. I want to stay even though my son is waiting. Because when I leave, you'll be alone."

"I've been alone my whole life. No one but you has ever set foot in my home. I don't regret keeping to myself, nor do I regret inviting you here." He gestured with his chopsticks, trying to articulate what Rakurai's company meant to him. "Your soul shines so brightly, that when you leave, darkness will fall. But I'm better for having met you. If the alternative was not to be caught by the rafeet, or to let you cross the bridge... I would take neither option. I promise that I will watch over you and your son. And ever look forward to your next visit."

It was a declaration that, maybe, he shouldn't have made. Not at a moment when they were about to part.

Rakurai didn't answer him with words. He leaned over the table and pressed a kiss to the corner of Tenzen's mouth. "My mind isn't made to forget. And I will come back."

They didn't linger after they'd finished their tea. Rakurai dressed and gathered his pack before he joined Tenzen in the gravel garden.

Tenzen held out a carefully shaped stone on a leather thong. "Keep that with you at all times," he said as he settled the amulet around Rakurai's throat. "It is obsidian…"

"Stone of protection and healing."

"It will guarantee you my aid should you need it."

"Tell me."

"Shinigami may enter the human realm for two reasons. To answer the call of a soul, and to avenge a desecration of our shrines."

"You have a shrine?"

"I will have if you set this piece of obsidian in a circle of stone and call my name."

Rakurai's eyes glowed. "I can… summon you to me?"

"If someone has desecrated my shrine, my appearing before them won't be pretty. Use it at need." He leaned and caught Rakurai's lips in a savage kiss. Then he opened the veil and watched Rakurai step through.

Tenzen's home had been his refuge for so long, he'd not considered that bringing Rakurai here would change how he saw it. As Rakurai's presence faded, the familiar space lost its welcoming serenity and grew empty and cold. He tidied with a wave of his hand, then wondered if erasing all sign of him and Rakurai together was a mistake. What if Rakurai never returned?

Don't think like that. He promised to visit and he's a man of his word.

He wandered from room to room, recalling snatches of conversations, exchanges of views, shared laughter... novel experiences for a reclusive death god that had proven addictive. For the first time in his life, he'd wanted another man's company, and he hadn't denied himself.

Maybe he should have asked. Or not kept Rakurai to himself for as long as he had, even if he'd salved his conscience by watching over Rakurai's son.

There'd been a moment, after he'd admitted that it was mid-winter in the human realm, that Rakurai had been truly angry.

Tenzen traced the panes in the shoji screen with his fingertips. It had been his fault that Rakurai had felt that he'd neglected his duties. If he wanted to make sure Rakurai returned to him, he had to remember that. He couldn't trust to Rakurai being so accepting a second time.

Rakurai? He whispered the word, not wanting to intrude on Rakurai's other life.

Rakurai replied without delay. *You could have warned me it's snowing here. I stepped right into a drift.*

Tenzen's mood lightened. He thinned the veil just enough to see Rakurai on the road leading to his manor, knee-deep in snow. *It's not my fault if you don't watch where you put your feet.*

As if I could have put them anywhere else. Besides, I was distracted. How about you?

I'm not distracted. He wouldn't admit that he was just discovering how it felt to be lonely. *In fact, I'm heading to my garden. A chat with the rafeet that trapped me is long overdue.*

Should I feel sorry?

For me?

Rakurai chuckled. *Hardly. I shall imagine you stern and unyielding. But what are you hoping to learn?*

I've never seen a rafeet link the power of its spawn into a net. Tenzen put his disquiet into words. *I want to know where it learned how to do so.*

PART 2
HUMAN REALM

BACK TO BACK

The shuffle and slap of bare feet on wooden boards filled the dojo. Rakurai defended, while Raijin whirled and attacked, advanced and retreated. He was graceful and light on his feet, and he fought with an eye to the main chance.

"Hands!" Rakurai warned when Raijin overreached, slashing downwards to take advantage.

Raijin yanked his hands out of reach just in time. He drew them high over his head, elbows wide, and struck the moment Rakurai recovered from his failed lunge and planted his feet.

The bamboo sword whacked Rakurai's thigh.

Raijin jumped back, grinning. "Four!"

Two more, and Raijin would earn himself an afternoon free from work. Judging by the sweat soaking Rakurai's robe despite the breeze blowing through the open screens and the fact that Raijin was doing most of the work, he wanted those hours of freedom.

"Fighting you is no longer simple," Rakurai acknowledged as they moved back into position.

"Your own fault. You're teaching me."

"Are you suggesting I teach you badly to make my own life easier?"

Their swords met with a crack like thunder. Raijin disengaged and whirled out of reach rather than answer. But the grin hadn't left his face.

He earned another point when Rakurai took a heartbeat too long to shift his weight and battled fiercely for the last hit.

Rakurai! Tenzen's voice was tight and sharp with urgency. Then the veil parted in the centre of the dojo. "I need your help!" The shout echoed through the room as well as Rakurai's mind.

Rakurai spun, saw Raijin three steps away, sword poised for his next attack and his gaze glued to the scene beyond the veil.

Heavy rain lashed a muddy field, where a lone figure battled half a dozen opponents. Unmoving shapes suggested they were the last members of a larger attack force. Tenzen wielded both whip and sword, but neither one with his usual grace. And a second group of attackers had appeared like a mist-shrouded threat at the edge of the field.

There was no time for preparations. Rakurai dropped the shinai and turned towards the gash in the veil, trusting that Tenzen could find him a sword.

"Father!" Raijin's eyes were wide, his expression pleading. He knew better than to delay Rakurai. Or ask to accompany him. "Be careful."

Rakurai found a smile. "I'll be back soon," he promised, and jumped through the gap.

"You should have called me sooner," Rakurai complained three hours later as he half-carried the Shinigami into his garden. "Just look at yourself." He helped Tenzen to a convenient seat, bracing him against his shoulder to make sure he stayed upright. The scent of roses perfumed the warm air—a world of difference from the winter-cold, rain-drenched field where they'd just fought.

The contrast of his bare, muddy feet on lush grass made Rakurai wish for a bath, but this indulgence had to wait.

Tenzen needed healing.

A demon's claw had opened the right side of his face from temple to jaw, just missing his eye. Bloody patches stained his tattered robe, and he held his right arm rigidly to his chest to avoid moving the broken collarbone.

"You were with your son," Tenzen wheezed. He released the souls he'd been defending into the soft air of his garden, and then slumped against Rakurai as if his duty had been the only thing holding him upright. "I didn't want to—"

"How many times must we have this discussion?" Rakurai tore strips off his hakama to fashion a sling for Tenzen's arm.

Annoyance, guilt, and worry formed a combustible mix in his gut. Tenzen had no qualms to call for his help while Rakurai was travelling or on missions for the Custodia. He refused to do so when Rakurai was at home with his son unless the situation was dire.

"Where else are you hurt? Anything serious?"

"Nothing that needs your attention. Sit down, Rakurai, please."

Rakurai was too anxious to sit. He ran his gaze over Tenzen's form, looking for rips and gashes in his clothes, for stains that showed red rather than shades of brown. He'd find a field of bruises under the shredded fabric of Tenzen's robes once he got them off the stubborn man. But he knew he had to wait until the worst of Tenzen's hurts were mended.

"Rakurai."

He sat with a sigh, watching the breeze stir the flowers, and the dance of the kaleidoscope of butterflies. "You worried me," he said when he could control his voice. "This time, you worried me. You carried too many souls to fight efficiently, yet you didn't call until your strength was almost gone."

The moment the veil had opened in the centre of his dojo, Rakurai had sensed that Tenzen was in trouble. The feeling had been so strong, he'd not even taken the time to find his boots. He'd jumped into the fight barefoot and furious, like one of the barbarians in the stories of old. And had arrived in the Otherworld to see Tenzen be hurt.

"I don't want to lose you."

Tenzen's hand found his and he twined their fingers. "You won't lose me. I'll always be here. But your time with your son is limited, you told me that. He's growing and changing, and you are away on Yuvine business enough as it is. I don't want to—"

Guilt lay like a freezing lump in Rakurai's stomach. "You're important to me, too. You deserve an equal share of my time and attention."

"It's not a competition, and I'm not complaining." Tenzen's voice was stronger. "I'm grateful for the time we have."

"You shouldn't have to be *grateful*. I should—"

Tenzen pulled his face around and kissed him. He smelled of sweat and blood and tasted of salt and metal, but as Rakurai dove deep, he found the familiar heat and sweetness. He clung to that, reminding himself over and over that Tenzen was safe.

"Let's not fight over things we can't change," Tenzen suggested when they drew apart. "I think I'm ready to move. Will you head back, or do you wish for a bath first?"

"I'll see you home," Rakurai said firmly, aware nothing had changed. "And join you in the bath."

"Stop fussing!" Tenzen admonished while Rakurai scrubbed the blood off Tenzen's skin and worked soap into his long hair.

"As if you're any better," Rakurai shot back.

Tenzen chuckled. Rakurai was right and—after years of fighting demons and dealing with the aftermath—they both knew it. "Which reminds me. Why were you barefoot?"

"I was sparring with Raijin when you called for me. It seemed urgent."

Tenzen wanted to deny it, but he knew he couldn't have held out until Rakurai had dressed and armed himself. Weighed down with hundreds of souls he'd gathered on a battlefield, he'd come as close to losing them all as he ever had. "I'm growing careless," he grumbled, more to himself than to Rakurai, as he climbed into the soaking tub. Rakurai settled beside him and, for the first time that day, Tenzen felt he could breathe.

"Careless how?" Rakurai asked after a while.

"Before I met you, I wouldn't have dared to bring back that many souls at once," he admitted. "I would have saved as many as I could while still fully able to fight. I would have made several trips if I needed to."

"And you've changed the way you work because of me?"

"Partly. Knowing that you'll help if I need it makes a difference. Or maybe it makes me lazy."

Predictably, Rakurai ignored the negative talk. "What's the other reason?"

"That the crowds of demons swarming each disaster are growing larger. You've seen it yourself. It's a feeding frenzy. If I left to deposit the souls in my garden—even if I just released them and hurried back right away— hundreds would die and lose their chance of another life." Tenzen closed his eyes and tried to block out the memories. "I'm not prepared to do that."

"So you gather and gather until you're too overburdened to fight. How do the other death gods handle this? We've seen more demon attacks in the last few years than in four centuries before. Surely you all face the same problem."

Tenzen shifted in the hot water, wincing when his newly healed side complained. "I don't know," he admitted. "We don't speak often."

"Maybe you should start." Rakurai closed his eyes and leaned his head against the padded rim of the bathing tub. "Cooperation," he muttered. "Humans cooperate. Even the Yuvine have started to learn to work together. Maybe the Shinigami need to take a leaf out of the human world's book."

"Perhaps." Tenzen couldn't imagine it. The seven Shinigami were spread wide across the Otherworld. They gathered souls in the human realm and tended their gardens. Would any of them choose to go to another Shinigami's aid when it might leave their own gardens unprotected?

He didn't voice his thoughts. Rakurai would be gone in too short a time and Tenzen didn't want to argue. He reached for the tray of food on the corner of the tub, intent on finishing the healing that Rakurai's lightning and his garden had begun.

And then, in a move that had become a habit, he thinned the veil and watched Raijin. The younger Yamakage knelt on the engawa, in the place where Rakurai liked to take tea. A tea set occupied the table beside him, but Raijin was not relaxed. He started at the smallest sound, and his eyes darted from the garden to the veranda and back.

"You need to return to the human realm," Tenzen said, voice as calm as he could make it.

Rakurai surged upwards in the hot water, caught sight of Raijin on the other side of veil, and then turned his head to regard Tenzen. "You're throwing me out?"

"Never. You're welcome here whenever you want to join me."

"I've joined you now."

"Your son saw you jump into the middle of a battle without bothering to find your shoes. Don't you think you should—?"

Rakurai's hands curled into fists and Tenzen thought he could hear his molars grind against each other. "I wish I could grab Raijin and come live in the Otherworld," he bit out, rising from the water and vaulting the edge of the tub.

The comment startled Tenzen so much he paid no heed to the expanse of smooth, wet skin in his line of sight. The thought of Rakurai living in the Otherworld with him took his breath. "Why don't you?"

Rakurai stilled, the drying cloth dangling from his fingers. "I'd be forsaking my clan and my duties."

Tenzen laughed. "Yes, I can see you sitting on the veranda all day, drinking tea."

"I'd be giving up my official duties as a Yamakage clan hunter," Rakurai clarified with a touch of impatience. "Of course I wouldn't stop fighting. I'm still a Yuvine and bound by Jumon's rules."

Tenzen lost his smile while he thought. "It seems to me that you value Jumon's rules over those of your clan."

"That's always been true. And has become more so since I met you. But I cannot make Raijin's choices," he said slowly. "What if I cut all his ties, take him away from the clan, the Custodia, and even the human realm... and he hates being here?"

"He may not. Hate it, I mean."

"I know. But choosing for him would be wrong."

"You could ask him and let him choose for himself."

"He's too young."

"Is he?" Tenzen contemplated that while Rakurai dressed. "I can make sense of human ages, but the Yuvine have always been a riddle to me in that regard. Raijin's seen a hundred and twenty years. A human would be dust and ashes, and he's not old enough to know his mind?"

"One hundred and fourteen," Rakurai corrected automatically. He'd stopped what he was doing and stared out across the garden, pensive as he often was when Raijin was the topic of their discussion.

"You always say 'when Raijin is grown'. What does that actually mean to a Yuvine?"

"A Yuvine who's of age is an available resource for their clan. The moment I sign Raijin's declaration, he can serve as a clan hunter or join the Custodia," Rakurai said. "For me, Raijin being of age means that he's completed his studies, has seen more than the manor and has been exposed to other parts of the Yuvine world. He'd still be incredibly young, but at that point I trust him to choose according to his own beliefs rather than to please me."

Tenzen had watched Raijin often enough over the last years to know that he enjoyed the learning. He studied sciences, history, politics, and languages, along with all the skills a Yuvine hunter had need of. He was young, yes, and Rakurai was right in thinking that Raijin aimed to please him, but when the two of them debated, Raijin expressed opinions of his own. And when they trained, he almost matched his father.

By Rakurai's definition, though, he wasn't yet of age. Tenzen quashed tendrils of disappointment and forced his voice and expression to remain calm. "You'd better go." He nodded at the image of Raijin. "I don't like to see him so fearful."

Rakurai shoved his feet into the boots Tenzen had set out for him and tied the sash on a clean robe. Then he stepped around the tub and leaned over Tenzen.

They kissed in this upside-down fashion, the ends of Rakurai's hair trailing in the water, and his palms tight on Tenzen's cheeks. The pains in Tenzen's body stopped to matter while they touched. Even the ache in his heart was easier to ignore.

"You will rest until you're fully healed?" Rakurai asked as he let go.

"I promise."

"And you will continue to speak to me?"

"I will speak to you. I will watch over you, and I will welcome you to my home and my garden when you're at leisure to visit." Tenzen repeated what he'd said thousands of times before, but he kept his eyes on Raijin and didn't watch as Rakurai stepped through the veil.

"Father!" Raijin jumped up when he caught sight of Rakurai, nearly oversetting the tea table. "Are you well?"

"I'm not hurt." He crossed to Raijin's side and wished he'd made it a habit to hug his son. Leaving both the people he most cared about in the same day played havoc with his heart. "Luck favours me, it seems. Are you making tea?"

"Yes." Raijin straightened the low table and the two cushions beside it. "Why is luck involved?"

"Because when I left the Otherworld, it was early morning. Time runs differently on the other side of the veil," Rakurai explained.

"I've read about that. Yamakage Hourin-sensei writes that time and seasons used to be aligned in both worlds, but that they're drifting apart at a faster rate each year."

"He's right. When I started serving in the Custodia, we could step back and forth across the veil and never notice a difference. These days, I can never tell at what time I'll arrive. Now. Tea?"

"Give me a few moments."

Rakurai folded himself onto a cushion. He watched his son warm the teapot before he carefully measured out the tea, each movement as sure as Rakurai's would be if he performed the task.

"You've done this a lot," he realised.

"Every day when you're away," Raijin admitted. "Hakkun-sensei complained that I never stopped working and didn't allow myself proper time for contemplation. So now, when I finish my training for the day, I make tea." He poured water into the pot and fragrant steam swirled between them. "Did you... manage to help your friend?"

Rakurai didn't want to remember the previous hours, but Raijin deserved an answer to his question. "He's alive. The demons are dead."

Raijin turned his attention from making tea and contemplated Rakurai. "He was hurt? Why didn't you stay with him?"

He should have. But Tenzen, who rarely asked for anything, had asked him to put Raijin first. "I saw to his wounds before I left. I didn't want you to worry. You're alone often enough. And I—"

"But that is our duty," Raijin protested. "To stand ready to fight when there is need. I would never complain about that."

Rakurai took the teacup Raijin handed him. "I know you're nothing like your cousins," he teased. "But is it so hard to believe that I would rather spend time with you than leave you here alone all the time?"

The flush on Raijin's cheeks didn't come from the light of the setting sun, or the fresh breeze. The embarrassed little smile he sent Rakurai's way made that quite clear.

Two Plus One

Rakurai settled himself more comfortably on the branch and rested his back against the oak's trunk. The dense canopy and a light breeze tempered the sweltering summer heat. Beneath him, Raijin darted across the meadow armed with whip and lightning.

"Left!" Rakurai shouted. "Rafeet."

Raijin dodged the imaginary attack. His whip snaked out. The cord wrapped around the trunk of a young pine, curled tight, and sliced the top third off the tree. Then he held out his free hand and shot a ball of lightning at the remainder of the trunk, obliterating it.

Deftly done, Tenzen's voice sounded in his mind.

Rakurai smiled. *You've returned from your errand? How long have you been watching?*

Only a short while.

You're home?

I'm home. All the souls are safe. And you've been busy.

"Hyeshi!" Rakurai called, testing Raijin's aerial defence. *I don't have much time left to train him. He's coming of age, whether I want to accept it or not.* "Rafeet!"

Raijin didn't hesitate. He darted in and out of the trees, miming attacks on flying demons, then sprinted into the centre of the meadow, lightning bolts clearing the way.

He's almost as fast as you.

Rakurai wanted to purr with delight. *I think he's actually faster. But don't tell him I said so. I don't want him to grow conceited.*

Little chance of that with you around.

I'm not that strict a teacher.

You're relentless. And sparing of praise.

"Sehr gut!" Rakurai called down to his son, smiling.

"Muy bien," Raijin replied promptly. "Molto bene. Very good."

Raijin was studying European languages in preparation for his first stint at the Custodia, and they'd been turning his practice into a game. Rakurai would offer a phrase in one language and Raijin would return it in the languages he was learning.

Did I mention relentless?

It's good practice for him, and amuses us both, Rakurai defended himself as he rose from his branch and prepared to descend to the meadow. *We'll speak later?*

We will. I need sleep.

Rakurai disliked when Tenzen disappeared from his mind with such abruptness. Too often it meant that he was hurt and hadn't taken the time to rest and recuperate in his garden. Maybe tonight, when Raijin was asleep, he could check on his lover. First, though—

He landed on the ground in a cloud of dust and took in Raijin's drooping shoulders and sweat-soaked robe. They'd been working since dawn, sparring sessions and mock combat drills using regular weapons and the lightning and weather that were Raijin's gift. Even without the strength-sapping heat it was a demanding schedule and Raijin had almost reached his limit.

"Let's call a halt," Rakurai decided. "You've done well. And we both deserve a bath and a leisurely meal."

"In six languages, no doubt," Raijin mock-grumbled around a large smile.

Rakurai returned the smile. Raijin had grown from an enthusiastic, uncertain youth into a young man. He'd retained his slim physique and delicate features, but his shoulders and arms had filled out and he'd earned his first battlefield scars the previous winter. He'd studied diligently, too, had languages and scientific facts at his fingertips. And he'd honed his gift to a razor-edged weapon.

Rakurai was proud of his son. "Maybe tonight you should choose the topics for conversation," he said, and Raijin's eyes went wide.

Tenzen was right. It was time that Rakurai acknowledged the progress Raijin had made. His son was a hunter. Whatever situation he found himself in,

Raijin would fight with courage and decisiveness. He'd earned Rakurai's respect.

See? I can offer praise, he told Tenzen, knowing the Shinigami wouldn't hear his admission, and turned to walk back to their home with Raijin by his side.

Tenzen returned to his garden, knowing he'd just escaped an argument. Rakurai had a nose for trouble, and Tenzen's need to see Rakurai had been greater than his desire to have his wounds mended.

Their first meeting had been chance. To Tenzen's surprise, their connection had endured, though their time together had grown less peaceful.

Rakurai's clan council sent him on mission after mission, leaving him hardly enough time to train his son. Tenzen's calls for help had become more frequent. And the clumsy, half-hearted attempts on Rakurai's life—that Rakurai refused to waste time investigating—had never quite let up.

They led lives filled with hardships, danger, and exertion with just hours spent in each other's arms to make up for them.

Tenzen wanted more time with Rakurai. He wished he could join the Yuvine in the human world and make their arrangement more of a two-sided bargain, just as he wished he could meet Rakurai's son.

Both wishes were daydreams. Rakurai had never offered to bring Raijin on one of his visits and Tenzen had never asked. And Shinigami had only limited access to the human realm.

He wouldn't complain, though. His life had become vastly more interesting since he'd met Rakurai.

He wandered his garden, letting his wounds heal, while the souls flocked to him for reassurance, to share a new insight, or to unburden themselves.

A pine forest, the air rich with the bitter scent of resin, was a new addition to his domain. Tenzen scrutinised it in passing, trying to spot the soul who'd created it.

The next corner that caught his eye—a riot of silver-leafed plants and white flowers that would no doubt look fabulous under moonlight—reminded Tenzen of Rakurai's love of sitting in his garden at night.

He circled a lake and crossed a bridge that hadn't been there earlier that day, until he reached the section of garden he'd been aiming for.

A carpet of heather and low brush dissolved into a desert of rocks, sand, and spindly cacti, which clung to life through sheer stubbornness. Once every few years, it rained. And then this arid, near lifeless desert would bloom.

Tenzen spent much time in this corner of his garden. The souls of rafeet, krull, hyeshi, and lesser demons tended to settle in this area, as if they were too afraid of the lush spaces his other souls created. These were the souls that most concerned him, who most needed his help.

Often, their behaviour puzzled him.

In his experience, rafeet didn't *recognise* the creatures they hunted. But when he'd called Rakurai from his dojo to help him fight a group of demons, one of the rafeet had done just that. It had stopped mid-attack, stared at Rakurai, and had backed away.

Too busy defending Tenzen, Rakurai hadn't noticed. But Tenzen had, and the soul of that strangely behaving rafeet was now in his garden.

Tenzen sat on the ground, his robes pooling around him, and sank into stillness. He listened as the souls whispered to each other, sharing tales of blood and war, of terror and fear. The whispers formed a crimson shroud, a fog of emotions Tenzen needed to absorb and clear to reach the memories. It was slow, demanding work, and Tenzen tackled it whenever he could.

He opened his eyes hours later, exhausted and none the wiser. The soul of the rafeet who'd seemed to recognise Rakurai had proved elusive, not yet ready to answer his call.

Yamakage Jumon had spent his time pondering the nature of the veil. Tenzen was more interested in understanding the nature of the darkness that surrounded the worlds and how souls came to be reborn in that space.

Like all the demon souls he'd brought to his garden, his newest arrivals had no memories of the time before they'd arrived in the Otherworld. All they retained of the place where they'd been reborn was terror.

Taking a soul's memories hampered its journey to a new life. Replacing its memories with nothing but fear was a harsh punishment on top of an already cruel fate.

Tenzen was determined to find out why souls were reborn in the darkness beyond the veil. He'd learn how those souls lost their memories. And once he knew, he'd put a stop to it.

He was a death god.

He was immortal.

And he was exceptionally good at waiting.

In Rakurai's parents' home, the evening meal used to be long and lavish, and shared with all the family's staff and retainers. When Rakurai and Naomi had set up their own household, they'd kept dinners small and intimate. Once the kitchen staff had placed the dishes, everyone was dismissed for the night to do as they chose.

Rakurai had retained the practice after Naomi's death, thinking it important to share every meal he could with Raijin. It was a way to reconnect with his son after his absences. To find out what Raijin had been learning and what he thought about.

Rakurai had never asked what their quiet dinners meant to his son, but he'd seen Raijin's disappointed expression often enough to know that he enjoyed sharing food with his father.

That night, their steward had laid dinner indoors as dark clouds massed along the western horizon offering the promise of much-needed rain. The screens stood wide in the hope of a breeze to combat the oppressive heat. The sunken fireplace in the centre of the dining room lay empty, but the inviting scent of smouldering charcoal rose from the grill to perfume the air. The cook had filled trays with thinly sliced strips of meat and vegetables, ready to be cooked over the coals. Rice, pickles, and sauces completed their meal, along with flasks of sake.

It was a dinner such as adults would share, and Rakurai thought that Raijin was making a point. He'd even chosen to wear a haori, though they never dressed formally for dinner unless they were entertaining guests.

"I know you're grown, Raijin," he said as they took their places at the table. "You don't have to prove it to me."

"Maybe I have to prove it to myself."

Rakurai had notified the Yamakage clan council that afternoon that Raijin had completed his studies. Now he reached for the bottle steeping in a water bath and poured two cups of sake. "Don't ever doubt that you've earned your new status," he said, offering a cup to Raijin. "I wouldn't declare you of age if you weren't ready."

They drained their cups as one, smiled like conspirators, and set about their dinner.

"Will you tell me about the Custodia, Father?" Raijin asked when they'd sated their first hunger. "Maru bet me that I'm going to make as much of a fool of myself as Hideki. I want to prove him wrong."

The Custodia was one of the few topics Rakurai had refused to discuss in anything more than general terms until Raijin was of age. "When did he tell you that?"

"Elder Daisuke sent him with the orders for your last mission, don't you remember?" Raijin shrugged. "No, probably not. You were gone so fast, you may not have seen him."

"I would have avoided him if I had. Why did you even talk to him?"

"I needed news. And do you know? He wore a frock coat and vest. And a shirt collar so high he could barely turn his head!"

Serving at the Custodia's Capri base had exposed a handful of the younger Yamakage to European fashions, and they showed them off whenever they could, much to the dismay of their elders. Rakurai, who wore frock coats and top hats when he travelled in Europe, had made sure Raijin knew how to dress appropriately. "How did he look?"

"Like a silly little boy playing dress up—without understanding what he was wearing."

"As long as he wasn't wearing his sandals on his head."

Raijin snickered. "I don't think he's as stupid as that. His tie was disgraceful enough. And the stuff he said about Hideki! Why ever did Elder Daisuke send *him* to the Custodia?"

There was something in Raijin's tone that brought Rakurai's head up. "What did he say to you?"

Raijin kept his eyes on the strip of meat he was turning on the griddle. "That Hideki was performing my duties because I was failing in my studies."

"Maru's talking out of his arse. You don't need me to tell you this. Daisuke wanted me here, so we had to send another hunter to the Custodia. And Daisuke chose Hideki because the little toad was scheming and making trouble. It was a punishment rather than a promotion, and he promptly disgraced himself."

"How? He's been there for a few years. Would they keep him if he was that much of a liability?"

"He's too conceited to— No. Let me tell this in order," Rakurai said and refilled their cups. "You know the Custodia is an outpost humans can visit when they need our help. The Custodia is also a place where hunters from all clans can train together. Hunters work mostly alone, so having somewhere to exchange views and learn new skills is helpful." He sipped his sake. "At least, that's how I find it. Your time there will be as useful to you as you make it."

"What about living there? Do we really have to sleep underground?"

"The base is on an island called Capri, just off the Italian coast. It's a place of lemon groves and stunning sunsets. But yes, sleeping quarters and training facilities are inside a cliff. The base is designed to keep us hidden from any but the humans who know about the Yuvine."

"And Hideki?"

"Hideki looks down on the humans and refuses to work with other Yuvine. It doesn't make him popular."

"That must have hurt," Raijin said, grinning.

Rakurai choked on a laugh. "It's challenging to live in such proximity with strangers. Much will be unfamiliar to you. I suggest you treat it as an opportunity, and if it gets too much, just go wave-running."

Raijin's eyes grew wide. "I'm not sure I even remember how to do that," he blurted, and then averted his gaze.

Rakurai knew why. Naomi had loved wave-running. She'd started to teach Raijin as soon as he could walk. And they'd neither practised it nor spoken of it since her death. "Don't apologise," Rakurai said. "She was your mother. You have a right to know her, and you can ask me anything."

Raijin didn't make him wait. "Was she a watcher?"

"Maru again?"

"Hm. He seems to know more about our family than I do."

"I owe you an apology for that. I... I didn't find it easy to speak of her, and I didn't want to distress you."

His bond with Naomi had lacked the passion he felt for Tenzen. But they'd been good friends and comfortable in each other's company. They'd created Raijin. And Rakurai could never regret that.

"And yes, your mother could sense demon activity on either side of the veil. That's how we found your grandparents after they were ambushed. Commander Tan Hao thinks that dedicated hunter/watcher teams might give us an advantage dealing with the increase in demon attacks."

"Will they?"

"I don't know. The only time I've tried it..." Rakurai rose, not wanting to remember the blood-soaked days and the grief that had come after. He pushed the screen door wider and watched as fat droplets of rain pelted the garden. In the clouds above him, Raijin, God of Thunder, rode the storm with rumbles and flashes. And behind him the younger Raijin, named for the Thunder God, laughed aloud.

When Rakurai turned he flicked his fingers and sent a small ball of lightning surging toward his father. Rakurai dodged and Raijin sent a second and then another, until Rakurai recognised the invitation to play.

He sent a ball of lightning back the way it had come, and Raijin rolled smartly out of the way, took cover behind a low table, and returned the attack.

Before he knew it, Rakurai was laughing while they dodged around the room, throwing lightning at each other. It showed the level of Raijin's control that not a single wall was damaged, and it was a mark of his stamina that Rakurai was out of breath before Raijin was.

"I look forward to finding out how much I remember of wave-running," Raijin said as he slid down the wall beside his father, breathing hard and laughing. "No doubt everyone else will be better at it than I am." A ball of lightning the size of a pea bloomed on the tip of his finger. "But I dare them to beat me at *this* game."

PUNISHMENT

Winter came early, with heavy snowfalls blanketing the countryside, and it lasted well into the following year. Tenzen studied the demon souls in his care and kept an eye on Rakurai, Raijin, and Elder Daisuke.

Never before had Tenzen watched the human realm, or the doings of the Yuvine, with such attention. It didn't bring enlightenment. Yamakage Daisuke, petulant and demanding, remained an enigma.

He wasn't Jumon, who'd commanded silence just by entering a room. Daisuke relied on favours, posturing, and the services of his secretary to get his way. He craved recognition and didn't seem to care that it was given only grudgingly.

"Politics," Rakurai said when Tenzen asked his opinion. "For as long as I've known him, he's traded favours, responded to flattery, and wanted everyone to acknowledge his position as elder."

Tenzen understood that. He didn't understand why he was having a tough time discerning Daisuke's gift when—as the eldest living Yuvine and head of the oldest Yuvine clan—Daisuke should have been radiating power. As it was, Raijin showed more potential while he slept than Tenzen sensed from Daisuke while the man was awake.

The dichotomy made him uneasy. And as winter turned to spring, he watched over Rakurai and his son with the unblinking attention of a cat watching over her kittens.

Ever since the Lugano Elder became advisor to the Christian pope, Daisuke has been insufferable, Rakurai said one night, when he had stopped at a roadside inn. He was returning home after yet another acrimonious meeting with the head of his clan, and all they could do was talk. *He wants to hold that same position with the Regent, and he wants my help—and everybody else's—to make it happen. All for the glory and fortune of the Yamakage clan, of course, with not a thought for himself.*

Since Tenzen had watched the meeting he knew of Daisuke's plans, but he'd learned that explaining a situation was Rakurai's way to rid himself of his anger when he couldn't meditate or practice sword forms. Tenzen didn't mind lending an ear or his support.

I cannot see how he means to achieve that aim. Or why he asked your help to do it. I suppose you could try to bribe the officials at the Imperial court, but… your honour is not that flexible.

It never was and never will be. All I can do is refuse and quote Jumon, but it hardly endears me to Daisuke.

You did offer him the option to appoint another hunter, Tenzen reminded him.

As if he'd ever send that useless nephew of his out of his sight, Rakurai scoffed. *He doesn't trust him as far as his shadow falls. Daitō is decorative. He has no usable skills.*

That's a touch harsh.

Not at all. He's arrogant. He trades on his relationship with Daisuke and manipulates those around him for his own gain. How can that help Daisuke curry favour with the Regent?

He stretched, almost toppling over when he compromised his balance. Tenzen grinned at the unusually clumsy move and took pleasure in watching the ripple of muscles across Rakurai's back. He wished he could do more than watch, though he would never say so. Wouldn't admit how much of a difference having Rakurai in his life had made to his existence. Rakurai had tempered a level of loneliness that Tenzen hadn't even been aware of.

You should sleep, he suggested when Rakurai yawned for the fifth time. He wanted to continue talking, but he knew that long hours of travel would fill Rakurai's day as they'd filled the last two.

I wish I could do more than sleep, Rakurai echoed Tenzen's thoughts as he settled on his mat. *I miss your touch. Miss our time together.* He left unsaid what Tenzen already knew, that disappearing into the Otherworld so close to Daisuke's manor would invite suspicion and speculation.

There will be time for us to meet when you have returned home, Tenzen promised. *Now sleep, while I watch over you.*

Rakurai closed his eyes. "It's still not fair," he muttered, "that you can watch me, while I never get to see you unless we meet." He smiled as he said it, and soon his breathing evened out, and he slept.

Tenzen didn't take his eyes from the man who meant so much to him. They had never discussed their feelings, but they cherished the hours and days they spent together. And every time, they found it harder to part.

Relations between a Yuvine and a creature from the Otherworld were pretty much unheard of. Even association with humans was frowned upon by some of the clans. Insular, arrogant, and self-absorbed—the more Tenzen learned about the Yuvine, the less he liked what he saw.

Yamakage Jumon had been different. He'd been curious, bargaining for knowledge, not power. And he'd kept his promises.

Tenzen sometimes wondered how the worlds might have turned out, had he been able to convince Jumon not to die. Jumon had been a human past his prime when he'd come to the Otherworld and made his bargain. He'd been ancient when he'd decided to leave this life for the next. If Tenzen had been a little less understanding, a little less inclined to see Jumon's side, a little less accepting of Jumon's desire to move on… would Jumon have changed his mind?

The Unseen Power had sent the wrong Shinigami to bargain with Jumon. Tenzen cared more for the souls in his garden than he cared for the worlds they'd come from or moved to. He fought to protect his souls but rarely involved himself in arguments.

Jumon had seen that. He'd made Tenzen care more about Jumon's desires than his own.

Had Jumon foreseen that his descendants would interpret his rules to suit their ambition? That they'd break the promise he'd made in good faith? Or had he known that there would be Yuvine like Rakurai and his son, who followed the rules and kept the bargain whatever the cost?

Sudden movement caught his attention.

His gaze swept left to right until it settled on four human men, dressed head-to-toe in dark clothes, the better to blend into the background.

The innkeeper met them at the gate, and a sizable amount of money changed hands before he hurried away down the road, leaving the gate to the inn wide open.

Rakurai!

He did not stir, his breathing heavy and slow.

Rakurai! Wake up!

If Tenzen could have crossed into the human world, he would have been there in a flash, shaking his lover awake. Instead, he stared helplessly as the men approached the inn.

Rakurai's frequent yawns, the fumbling slowness of his movements—resembling those of a human who'd overindulged—and the money handed to the innkeeper now took on a different tint.

Had the man drugged Rakurai's food to ensure he slept through an attack? Were the intruders planning to rob one of the traders staying overnight or were they here for Rakurai?

His answer wasn't long in coming.

The men passed through the main room of the inn, ignoring the blanket-wrapped, snoring patrons. Once they reached the courtyard, they gathered on the veranda outside Rakurai's room.

Rakurai! Rakurai!

Tenzen screamed at the top of his mental voice, before he parted the veil close to his lover, almost close enough to touch. A shout would attract attention. Could he remain in the Otherworld while reaching for Rakurai? Could he shake him awake? Rakurai had succumbed to sleep before he'd had time to set up a shrine for Tenzen beside his sleeping mat, removing any chance of Tenzen coming to his aid.

Shadows moved beyond the squares of the screen door.

A hand stretched to slide it open.

And Tenzen ignored a lifetime of adhering to the rules and keeping to himself. He reached through the veil and shook Rakurai until his teeth rattled.

Rakurai woke with a jerk, but the subsequent slow, confused blink confirmed Tenzen's suspicions that Rakurai wasn't himself.

"Attackers outside your door," he hissed. "The innkeeper laced your dinner with a sleeping draught."

Rakurai struggled to his feet as the men burst through the door. He swayed, neither steady, nor coordinated enough for a fight against four, but he was holding his whip.

The space was too small for five grown men to manoeuvre, but the attackers' surprise at finding their target awake and armed gave Rakurai the chance to put the futon between them and plaster his back to the wall.

One of the men backed out of the room.

Tenzen marked him as he rounded the outside of the building, aiming for the door at Rakurai's back.

Rakurai.

I know.

Even Rakurai's mental voice slurred. His movements were sluggish, too, but he set his feet and gripped his whip, bracing himself for the attack.

The men rushed towards Rakurai.

Rakurai's whip hissed through the air.

Missed.

He swung again.

Missed once more.

The fourth man arrived on the other side of the thin screen, knife in hand.

Rakurai! Behind you!

Rakurai blinked. Alarm widened his eyes as the drugs in his bloodstream yielded to his finely honed sense of danger. He sidestepped one swinging fist. Brought up his whip to deflect a knife. Only to stumble backwards, into stabbing range of the man outside the garden door.

Drugged into near-compliance and caught between four attackers, Rakurai's life measured in moments.

Tenzen was done screaming warnings.

He stepped through the veil, sword in hand.

The blade pierced the rice paper of the garden door, reaching for the shadow beyond.

A gurgling groan announced it had found its target.

Rakurai's attackers froze as their comrade fell into the room, life streaming red from his body. It gave Tenzen the chance to plant a boot in one man's chest and kick him into the wall. The second man, a short, sturdy fellow, brought up his knife and faced Tenzen.

He can see me?

The knife thrust towards Tenzen's middle, answering that question. He twisted out of the way, cursing the delay. He used to pass humans unnoticed and now, when he was desperate to reach Rakurai's side, they saw him? The human attacked again, and Tenzen, out of patience, dropped low and buried his sword in the man's gut.

The man he'd kicked was back on his feet. He rushed Tenzen, now holding a knife in either hand.

Rakurai's whip shot past Tenzen and the supple cord wrapped around the man's neck. He dropped his knives to claw at his throat, giving Tenzen opportunity to thrust the blade into his heart.

A handful of heartbeats and the cool, quiet room had become a battlefield.

Tenzen didn't care. Only one more attacker stood between him and Rakurai. He yanked the sword free, spun… and found the last assassin far too close.

A gut punch drove him backwards.

Heat seared through his chest.

Tenzen staggered, heard a strangled shout, and didn't even raise his head. The pool of red spreading across the front of his robe commanded all his attention. *How did they see me? They were human. And how…?*

Pain hammered him then, confirming that the blood wasn't a mirage. A human who shouldn't be able to see or hurt him had driven a knife into his chest.

His knees buckled on a wave of weakness and Tenzen landed on the matting, gasping in pain.

Understanding dawned.

He had crossed into the human realm without a soul calling for him.

He had broken the rules.

This was his punishment.

SAVING A GOD

The room stank like a slaughterhouse. Blood slicked the tatami matting and splattered the torn shoji screen. Rakurai's bare feet slid in the mess, and the night air raised goosebumps on his skin. He suppressed a shiver, grateful that the chill helped dispel the fog that had slowed his movements and numbed his mind.

He remembered yawning more than his fair share over dinner and while he'd talked with Tenzen. Remembered stumbling over his own feet on the way to his futon. And then... nothing, though he was usually a light sleeper, aware of his surroundings even when he took his rest.

Waking with Tenzen staring at him in panic, and four strangers forcing their way into his room had been less scary than being unable to move with any kind of coordination. His whip had missed its target—twice!—though the men who'd attacked him had been mere feet away. And human.

Now three corpses marred the floor.

Tenzen knelt, an ever-spreading patch of red on his robe.

And Yamakage Daisuke's private secretary stared at him over a bloody knife.

His difficulties comprehending the situation gave him the clue he needed. "Drugs?" he slurred.

Yamato licked his lips. "We had to get close to you," he said. "I didn't dare fail again."

"Yet fail you did."

"Because of him," Yamato grated through his teeth. "He was not supposed to be here. He *wasn't* here. Who is he?"

Rakurai didn't bother with an answer. He wanted to call the lightning, turn Yamato into a patch of grease, but the inn's other patrons had no part in this feud. His rage gave him focus and he took Yamato's head with a single slash of the whip.

Yamato's head hit the ground first. It rolled a couple of times and then Yamato's body crumpled and collapsed on top of its head. More blood soaked the matting, but Rakurai was past caring.

He dropped the whip and fell to his knees by Tenzen's side.

The Shinigami was paler than Rakurai had ever seen him, his eyes wide with surprise. Tenzen's hands were icy cold when Rakurai laid his own over them, his blood hot on Rakurai's skin.

"Tenzen, talk to me."

"So stupid," Tenzen wheezed, bright red froth bubbling on his lips. "I wasn't... watching my back. I don't usually have to. Not here. With humans."

"Can you stand? I'm not... at my most sprightly, and... We need to get you through the veil."

"No."

"What do you mean, no? Tenzen, you're bleeding. You must—" The panic in his gut battled the blanket of fog in his mind. He had to act, and act fast before Tenzen lost too much blood, or a second wave of assassins arrived to finish what the first lot had started. So far, the inn was quiet, but Rakurai didn't bank on it remaining this way. He tried to stand, tried to pull Tenzen to his feet.

Tenzen resisted. "I can't leave here."

"Why not?"

"The men were human, Rakurai. They shouldn't have seen me."

Rakurai stilled. Tenzen was right. None of the men should have seen the Shinigami. And Yamato's knife shouldn't have hurt him.

"When we met, you told me that your elder sent you after the rafeet as punishment." Tenzen leaned forward, bracing himself with one hand on the matting, while other was pressed tight to his chest.

"I remember," Rakurai said. "What of it?" He tore strips from Yamato's hakama and folded them clumsily into pads.

"Shinigami aren't meant to cross the veil unless we're called by souls. I didn't wait for that call."

"You came to save me."

"You are alive. I broke the rules coming to your aid. My actions made me visible to the humans and vulnerable to their attacks."

"You think this is punishment?"

"Yes." Tenzen didn't fight when Rakurai pressed a thick pad of fabric over his wound and held it tight. He barely noticed what Rakurai was doing, too caught up trying to reason out what had happened. "I didn't think of it, since no human ever saw me before unless they stood on death's threshold."

Another wash of hot blood soaked the cloth. "Don't talk," Rakurai demanded. "Don't move."

Tenzen grasped his wrist. "I'm glad I came."

"I'm not. Look at the mess you've made of yourself." He pressed down harder. "Will this need stitches? Or will you heal as you do in the Otherworld?"

"Until I return to the Otherworld, I'm mortal."

"Does that mean you can die?"

"Yes."

"No. I'll not have it. What about… can I share my lightning?"

Tenzen's chuckle turned into a pain-filled grimace. "You'd burn me to a crisp. Punishment, remember? I have no magic. I can't cross the veil until I'm healed."

"That doesn't seem fair."

"I broke the rules. I must accept the punishment. It could have been worse."

"How?"

Tenzen's next breath turned into a bubbling cough. More blood gathered in the corners of his mouth. Rakurai wiped it away. His hands were steadier now, his mind clearer. Tenzen was hurt. If he was also mortal, then Rakurai had to treat him as he would treat an injured comrade. Get him out of this blood-soaked inn to a healer, and then somewhere safe where he could rest and recover.

Rakurai retrieved his pack. "Let me patch you up so you don't bleed out on the way." He tore up his haori, added another thick pad of cloth to the one already covering Tenzen's wound and secured both with bandages drawn as tight as he dared.

"On the way to where?" Tenzen whispered the question.

"A healer. Do you think you can walk?"

Tenzen considered. "I'll try. Should we…" He waved at the bodies.

Rakurai ignored the men, all his attention on helping Tenzen to his feet. "Leave them. Inept assassins don't deserve my respect." Then something occurred to him. "Will you need to guard their souls?"

Tenzen clung to the shoji screen to stay upright. "I have no powers. I cannot sense any souls, nor can I gather them and take them to my garden."

"What happens to souls who—?"

"Have no one to guide them to their next life? If they don't find their own way to the Otherworld or no other Shinigami hears their call, they'll perish."

"Good." Rakurai stared at his hands, crimson with Tenzen's blood. The rage inside him didn't yield to reason. And he wished the four were still alive, so he could kill them all over again. He couldn't even look at them without feeling a wild need for violence. At least their actions had had consequences.

He joined Tenzen on the veranda, offered him his shoulder to lean on. This time, Tenzen accepted and Rakurai's knees almost buckled in gratitude. Tenzen had put himself in harm's way to keep him safe. Rakurai would do nothing less.

POWERLESS

The shouts of a food vendor touting his wares in the street woke Tenzen from a nap. He had fallen asleep with the book he'd been reading still open on his lap, and he moved carefully now to work the kinks from his neck and upper back as he rose. The Western-style chair was an indulgence in a house furnished like Tenzen's own in the Otherworld, but he had to admit that he was sick of spending his days on a futon.

Rakurai had seen that long before Tenzen, and he'd gone out and brought back the chair without even discussing the matter.

"You'd never have asked," he'd said after two burly men had wrestled the chair through the genkan, the entrance hall, and into Tenzen's room.

He was right, too. Tenzen didn't get sick. Time in his garden healed all wounds and injuries. And, after everything Rakurai had done to keep him alive, he didn't want to make demands.

Tenzen had no memories of the healer who'd patched up his wound, nor could he remember the journey to the house Rakurai had found for them. He had no idea where they were, either, except that the street outside was busy from early morning until late at night and that—for the most part—the people were cheerful.

Bereft of his powers, Tenzen found the human realm difficult to navigate. The light was dimmer, the shadows deeper, and the air neither sustained nor revived him, turning food and drink from a much-loved indulgence into a necessity. Most of all, he missed conversing with Rakurai mind-to-mind. Sharing their thoughts had become such a habit that not being able to talk to Rakurai when he was out of his sight bothered him more than the healing wound.

When he'd first woken, he'd found Rakurai kneeling beside his futon, deep shadows under his eyes and lines bracketing his lush mouth. The lines hadn't been there before and Tenzen had set himself the task to make them vanish once more.

Without his powers, Tenzen healed as slowly as a mortal. But he found boredom and discomfort a small price to pay when he had Rakurai's company for an extended time. For far too long they'd only snatched days here and there. Keeping their liaison secret so Rakurai wouldn't attract more of Daisuke's animosity had seemed a logical choice at first. But as the seasons passed, Tenzen often felt that they deserved more.

Now he had more, though not in the way he'd imagined.

Fate was fickle that way.

He moved around the room, shaking off the last remnants of sleep. The food vendor, who'd ceased his shouting while serving a customer, picked up his chant again. Tenzen would have liked to step outside and sample the man's wares. He'd never interacted with living humans before. Unfortunately, his eyes were too noticeable to allow him to venture out when Rakurai had worked so hard to keep them hidden.

He was reaching to open the screens to the small courtyard garden, when footsteps hurried towards his room.

"Tenzen!" Rakurai burst through the door in a swirl of windblown hair and dishevelled robes.

"What is it? Is Raijin—?" After the attack on Rakurai, Tenzen had begun to fret more over the younger Yamakage than Rakurai himself. He'd told Rakurai more than once to head home and make sure Raijin was safe, but Rakurai had stubbornly clung to Tenzen's side.

"Raijin's safe," Rakurai now said absently. "I had a letter this morning." His gaze swept over Tenzen, the book on the chair, the closed screen door with its rice paper panes filtering the light. "You're safe."

Tenzen blinked. "I'm safe," he agreed. "What made you doubt that?"

"I thought I saw two of Daisuke's retainers. I feared…" He took a deep, shuddering breath and shook his head, lost for words.

Tenzen crossed the room and took Rakurai's hand. The fingers were icy cold to his touch. "They had you that worried?"

"You're injured. You were hurt protecting me. I don't want—"

"Shh." Tenzen stopped the torrent of words with his fingertips. "I'm safe. I'm recovered enough to fight if it comes to it. Which you'd know if you'd sparred with me as I asked."

"You cannot—"

"I've lost my powers, not my fighting skills. And I'm nearly healed. I wouldn't have…" He didn't quite know how to continue that sentence, since—without his powers—the extent of Rakurai's fears was hidden from him. "It's been a few years since you refused to kill the Lugano hunters. Do you really think your elder still harbours a grudge after all this time?"

"Daisuke lives to take offence. We argue every time I'm forced to meet him."

"Maybe. But with Yuvine hunters at his disposal, would he send humans after you? When he regards humans as lesser?"

Rakurai's tense shoulders relaxed a little. For the first time in far too long he gave Tenzen his weight. "You're right. It seems too ill-considered a move. But if Daisuke didn't send them, what was Yamato doing there?"

"Yamato… oh, the man who stabbed me."

"Daisuke's private secretary. He was also part of the group who ambushed me on the Nakasendo on the day we met."

"That was just after you refused to kill two Yuvine on Daisuke's orders. A case could be made for your elder being angry then." Tenzen tightened his arms around Rakurai, voicing thoughts he'd never spoken aloud. "I've never understood all these half-hearted attempts on your life. You're a Yuvine hunter. You're one of the most highly skilled fighters in the two worlds, and someone is sending *humans* to kill you?"

He felt Rakurai's startled surprise, the sudden indrawn breath.

"I didn't think."

"Neither did I. We dealt with the attempts when they happened and moved on with our lives. You never cared to find out more, and I didn't push you on it. Now… I may have a few souls to interrogate when I return to my garden."

Rakurai raised his head. His eyes, wider and darker than usual, reflected both surprise and awe. "You can do that? Talk to the souls you guard?"

"What do you think I do with my time, Rakurai? I prepare the souls for their next life. I teach them the skills they'll need and make them pay for sins committed in their previous life. And yes, interrogating them about their deeds is part of that."

"I never asked."

"And I'm not used to sharing such details." He pulled Rakurai close once more. "It's a pity I couldn't gather Yamato's soul. It would have been the easiest way to gain answers. Still… it's at least feasible he took orders from others beside Yamakage Daisuke."

"He never struck me that way. But it's as likely an option as me having offended someone else to the point they want me dead. Or as Daisuke having another reason for his animosity."

"And the answer is?"

"I don't know. I haven't quarrelled with anyone. As for Daisuke… He and I have never been cordial. He was a clan councillor when I was born, was clan elder before I came of age. We had very little to do with one another. Maybe my parents had a feud with him and I've inherited his dislike. It's something he might do. Transfer a grudge as other men transfer an allegiance, you know?"

"How did your parents die?"

Rakurai turned his head away and contemplated the screen door hiding the garden. "A rafeet ambushed them and tortured them to death," he whispered in the end. "Naomi and I were too late to save them."

Tenzen heard the pain and swallowed his questions. Daisuke couldn't have had a hand in *that* death. And those botched attempts on Rakurai's life didn't seem to fit his personality either.

"Could it be a warning?"

"I've thought of that. But what would they be warning me about? Or away from? In truth, it feels more like a distraction. Something designed to keep me looking over my shoulder. But for what reason?"

He stepped out of the circle of Tenzen's arms and started to pace the room. Tenzen watched, wishing he'd never started that discussion, and knowing they should have had it a long time ago. They'd both been indulging in make-believe, treating their time together like an enchanted oasis far from everyday strife. Until reality broke that enchantment.

"We should consult the Yuvine archives," he suggested. "If luck favours us, you might learn what rides your elder. Or who's trying to distract you."

"The Yuvine archives," Rakurai said. "If it weren't for my father mentioning them once, I wouldn't know they existed."

"Then let's make it our mission to explore as soon as I'm recovered enough to cross the veil. And meanwhile…" He reached for Rakurai, tilted his head up and kissed him, deep and hungry. He poured everything into the kiss: his frustration over the speed of his recovery, his need for touch and companionship, the strength of his desire for Rakurai.

Rakurai matched his ferocity, and when he guided Tenzen to the far side of the room, all Tenzen's earlier complaints about not wanting to spend any more time on a futon promptly disappeared.

"Let me do the work," Rakurai said, reaching for the sash of Tenzen's robe.

Tenzen bristled. "I'm fine. I can—"

"Please."

Rakurai stopped his next complaint with a kiss, and Tenzen didn't mind that at all. He wanted Rakurai's hands on him, and not in the solicitous, impersonal manner of a nurse. His healing was near complete, and it grated on him when Rakurai treated him like an invalid. He'd borne his slow recovery with stoicism, but his patience had grown thinner every day while Rakurai hovered, fretted, and tried to stop Tenzen from doing even the smallest thing for himself. Passion had had no place in Rakurai's ministrations, and his reluctance had tested Tenzen's temper.

Stop being annoyed, he admonished himself silently when he noticed where his thoughts had strayed. *Stop thinking. Be here. With Rakurai. Enjoy what you have.*

He focussed on the touch of Rakurai's lips, his questing tongue. Gave himself up to the heat building between them. And was glad that, while he moved with care, at least Rakurai wasn't stopping his work on Tenzen's sash.

Rakurai could be forceful in their lovemaking, and Tenzen had found that he enjoyed the tight clasps and rough thrusts, the finger marks and bruises he'd find afterwards on his skin. He wanted nothing more than for Rakurai to shove him into the nearest wall and take him hard and fast, but he knew it wouldn't happen.

Not this night. Because Rakurai could also be achingly tender, and as he unwound Tenzen's sash and parted his robe, he touched him with a gentleness that bordered on reverence.

He trailed his fingers from Tenzen's throat to his navel, and for a long, charged moment, their eyes met and held. Despite his age and the many battles he'd fought, Tenzen's skin had been without blemish. Now he bore a scar, a pink line two inches wide, a reminder of a blade sunk deep, and flesh newly knitted together.

"Will you keep this?" Rakurai whispered the question, his fingers hovering so close to his skin, Tenzen could feel their warmth.

"Most likely. It's a reminder of my punishment."

Rakurai leaned his head on Tenzen's shoulder. "For me it's a reminder that I can lose you, even though you're a god."

"Only if I break the rules." Tenzen slid his hands into Rakurai's long hair and pulled his head up. "And I only do that when your life's at stake."

"You're breaking the rules now. I told you to let me do the work tonight."

He sounded so indignant that Tenzen couldn't hold back a smile. "Then I suggest you stop stalling. I'm not made of glass, but I own I'm short of patience."

Rakurai narrowed his eyes, but he didn't argue. He made short work of Tenzen's robe, then sank to his knees to deal with the ties of Tenzen's hakama.

Had it been Tenzen's choice, he'd have taken a knife to the sturdy black fabric and its endless ties. He craved Rakurai's touch so much that every delay felt like torture, like another chance for his body to put his mind on the rack.

Rakurai sensed his desperation and didn't tease. And when the hakama succumbed to Rakurai's clever fingers and he bent his head to swallow Tenzen to the root, Tenzen finally stopped thinking and gave himself up to sensation.

"You're not healed enough to open the veil. Which tells me that you're not healed enough to step through it." Rakurai stood in the middle of the room, hands on hips and frowning. His long silver hair hung loose around his shoulders in vivid contrast to the dark blue of the kimono.

Tenzen tore his gaze away and pushed to his feet. He was done being treated like an invalid. Especially after the night they'd just spent.

"Has it occurred to you that I'll never be able to open the veil from this side?" he asked when he stood close enough to Rakurai that he could feel the heat radiating from his lover's body. "I have no powers here."

Rakurai's eyes went wide. "I hadn't… Does that mean you'd be trapped in the human realm if I wasn't with you? For all the years of your life?"

"It's punishment," Tenzen reminded him. "Though if you hadn't been here, I wouldn't have broken the rules and entered the human realm without cause. So, don't you see? It is your duty to return me to the Otherworld."

A corner of Rakurai's mouth quirked up. He took the last step separating them and fused his mouth to Tenzen's in a kiss they'd both been hungry for all morning.

"I'll open the veil," Rakurai said when they parted. "But if returning to the Otherworld does not restore you completely…"

"I'll spend time in my garden before we explore the archive," Tenzen offered a compromise. Anything for the chance to return home. Anything for a chance to find out who was targeting Rakurai, and why. "You could go and check on Raijin."

"Raijin is fine."

"So you keep telling me." The two Yuvine had exchanged regular messages while Rakurai watched over Tenzen's recovery. Tenzen had never written a letter in his life and hearing tiny snatches of Raijin's daily activities in this way intrigued him.

"As soon as your powers return we can watch him from the Otherworld."

"I've never seen you so reluctant to leave me," Tenzen teased.

"I'm always reluctant to leave either one of you." Rakurai slid his hands over the front of Tenzen's robe, tracing a long-vanished stain and a tear mended with tiny stitches. "I don't want to see you at death's door ever again."

"You know I can't promise you that."

"I know. I'll settle for you doing your best to stay safe."

Packing their belongings took little time. Rakurai left a note for the owner and closed and latched the shutters before he joined Tenzen on the engawa, the veranda that connected the house to the garden.

Tenzen's gaze roamed over the gravel swirls and rocks Rakurai had repositioned to suit his own taste, and the lush foliage that marked the edge of the small space. As every time, he noted the absence of butterflies. And he couldn't wait to check on his garden.

THOUGHTS AND MEMORIES

Fear slicked Rakurai's palms as he parted the veil. He knew little of death gods and the rules they had to follow. What if Tenzen's actions had cost him his powers forever? What if he couldn't return to the Otherworld?

Tenzen didn't share his misgivings. He smiled until the skin beside his eyes crinkled. "I can see the gash in the veil."

Rakurai's mouth fell open. "I… I hadn't thought of that," he admitted for the second time in as many days.

"Why should you? I didn't expect humans to see me until they did. We're slaves to our knowledge, whoever we are."

Rakurai wondered if the comment meant to hide Tenzen's nervousness, but before he could ask Tenzen stepped through the veil. Rakurai followed, the touch of sticky tendrils a familiar tug on his skin and hair.

He found his lover two steps away from the barrier, curled forward with both his arms wrapping his middle, supporting the healing wound. It was daytime, but darkness shrouded Tenzen's form, and Rakurai struggled to make out his features. Tenzen appeared to be trapped in smoke and Rakurai had no idea what to do.

"Tenzen! Tenzen talk to me."

Tenzen held up one finger, stopping Rakurai where he stood. "Give me... Just one... Heartbeat."

Air whistled through his teeth. With each breath, the darkness faded until the sight of him no longer hurt Rakurai's eyes.

Tenzen straightened. "*That* was not enjoyable. I hope it marks the end of my punishment."

He opened his palm and a butterfly appeared. It was a gorgeous specimen, with large, sweeping wings of a purple hue Rakurai had never seen in the human world. It rested on Tenzen's palm, wings moving lazily, in no hurry to be about its business.

Rakurai kept his eyes on Tenzen. For weeks he'd believed that the greatest danger to Tenzen came from the knife wound and the chance of infection. Tenzen had never once mentioned that the rules he had broken might lead to him being abandoned in the human realm.

How would Tenzen have lived, an age-old death god, without his powers?

Would he have become a draw for rafeet, krull, and other demons, while lacking the ability to defend himself against them?

What would have happened to his garden, and all the souls contained within it?

And what would have happened to them? Would he, the long-lived Yuvine, have had to stand by and watch Tenzen age and fade away?

"That was… so reckless," he stammered. "You should have…"

Tenzen released the butterfly and was beside him in an instant. He pulled Rakurai close and settled his palm on Rakurai's neck in a move that never failed to ground him. "I should have what?"

"Considered it. Told me. I… don't know."

"There was no time for consideration. You were in danger. I acted. I don't regret it," Tenzen's voice rumbled, low and soothing. "I'd do it again in a heartbeat."

"You will not!" Rakurai protested, but he clutched at Tenzen as if he wanted to hold on to him forever.

"I will if it is necessary. Some things are worth fighting for." He slipped two fingers under Rakurai's chin and lifted his face so he could kiss him. "You know that better than most," he said when they drew apart.

Rakurai didn't want to argue, even though he disagreed. Tenzen's life was more important than his own. But he couldn't dispute Tenzen's priorities or make his choices. "You had no idea that you would be punished."

"Not true. I knew there would be consequences. That I didn't know what those consequences were is beside the point. Now, let's go and explore the archive."

"There is just one problem," Rakurai said, indicating the featureless piece of land he'd brought them to. "I've no idea where the Yuvine archives are kept."

Tenzen burst out laughing. He had regained his proud stance and calm demeanour, a death god in all his glory and power. When he laughed, Rakurai wanted to worship the ground he walked on. Not that he'd admit to that when he was still angry with him for risking his life.

"I didn't think my comment was that funny."

"Maybe not. Fortunately for us, I know my way around the Otherworld." He reached for Rakurai and two heartbeats later they stood on a headland overlooking the ocean. Waves rolled below them. Salt spray peppered his skin while gusts of wind whipped his hair into tangles. And right in their line of sight, a tall lighthouse rose bright white against the gloom of the lowering clouds.

"This is the Yuvine archive?"

"Built by Yamakage Jumon himself. His thoughts and memories are right at the top of the lighthouse. They're the light you see shining out across the sea."

Rakurai reminded himself to close his mouth. "Have you read them?" he asked, awed by the very idea. "Jumon's records, I mean."

"He led a very long life," Tenzen replied, striding through the tall grass towards the lighthouse. "I've listened to some, but I've not been here in centuries. Back in Jumon's day, the Yuvine were worth listening to. These days… not so much."

"Listening? What do you mean?"

"This isn't an archive of written records, Rakurai. The archives store every Yuvine's thoughts and memories in giant scroll-filled halls. Entertaining for a few days here and there, but beyond frustrating if you're trying to find a specific event."

"*Every* Yuvine's thoughts?"

"Quite. I don't know how it's done. Only that finding anything in the place is a nightmare."

Rakurai followed in Tenzen's wake. Ahead of him, the lighthouse appeared to float in the air. He understood why as they drew close. A deep chasm split the headland, with the lighthouse positioned on a narrow spur. The only way to access the lighthouse was a flimsy-looking construct made from rope and knots that swayed and swung in the gusts coming off the sea.

"You couldn't have taken us right up to the door?"

"The headland is warded against all powers to ensure that nothing is removed from the archive. There are wards inside, too. Jumon made sure that not a single record can be erased or changed. Something about history being written by the victorious."

"You're a god, Tenzen. Do Jumon's strictures apply even to you?"

"Being a god doesn't absolve me from responsibility. The Unseen Power created this space for Jumon to build his archive and the Unseen Power protects it from damage."

"And I suppose that flimsy bridge has its own wards and protections?"

"You suppose correctly."

Tenzen set one foot onto the bridge and a thin mist drifted up from the chasm below. "It gets thicker the closer you get to the middle of the bridge. The wind picks up, too, so hold tight to the ropes."

He set off, and Rakurai had no choice but to follow.

The bridge was just wide enough to place his boots side by side. It swayed with each of Tenzen's steps and undulated sickeningly when Rakurai began to pick his way along its length. At least the ropes strung as hand guards were rough and reassuringly sturdy against his palms.

He tightened his grip when Tenzen disappeared into the mist, and then dropped his gaze to his feet, glad that he couldn't see what awaited him if he slipped.

A gust of wind hit him, and the bridge swung out wide.

Rakurai clung to the ropes and fought for balance. The fog obscured every landmark he could have used to orient himself, reduced his world to a wash of milky white that shook and shifted under his feet.

Tenzen!

Keep moving, came the familiar voice. Rakurai could have wept. They'd not spoken mind-to-mind since the night he'd been attacked at the inn. Hearing Tenzen's voice now was… Heat clogged his throat and he breathed through the lump. He was trapped on a flimsy rope over a gorge with waves dashing against the rocks hundreds of feet beneath him. He couldn't see where he was or where he was going. But Tenzen was nearby, and he wouldn't let him come to harm.

I'm ahead of you. Keep moving.

Rakurai did as he was told.

The stairs spiralled to the top of the lighthouse and down into the cliff, opening onto huge halls at every rotation.

Rakurai ventured into one of the gloomy halls. His footsteps echoed and it lacked enough light to make out the ceiling. Just as it lacked tables, chairs, lamps, and any other items he would expect to furnish an archive. Horizontal shelves, carved into the walls, held thousands of scrolls, each about as long as Rakurai's forearm and as wide as his wrist. "More scrolls than I can count, and not a label in sight."

"That's the problem with the archives. There is no index and no system to direct you to the memories you seek. The seals on the scroll cases are the only signs to guide us. They'll reveal from which clan the memories originate."

"So if the archive starts with Jumon's memories, everything in the lighthouse itself would be Yamakage?"

"Near enough. Jumon's memories occupy the upper stories. The memories of his contemporaries and those who lived in the centuries after his death fill the main part of the lighthouse. The Perkhon clan formed next and there are records from the Perkhon near the gate where we entered."

"If they're from the time when the Perkhon clan first arose, then going down should bring us closer to the present."

"That's what I've found, yes."

Rakurai set a foot on the spiral stairs and started to make his way deeper into the cliff. "Which means what we want should be near the bottom."

"That would be my conclusion also," Tenzen said and followed him down.

Ten thousand years of Yuvine history filled many storeys. Rakurai had no idea whether he stood above the level of the sea, or if the steps led into the seabed and beyond. The stairs wound deeper and deeper, but not in the way a normal spiral staircase would. Nor were the halls all of the same size. Larger, loftier ones, stretching deep into the hillside alternated with narrower, low-ceilinged rooms that Rakurai could barely stand in.

"Is there a reason why this has been built in such a lopsided fashion?" he queried after he'd bumped his head on the lintel coming out of one of the smaller rooms. The scrolls stored there were still old histories, long before Daisuke's birth. He skipped a few levels, trying to gauge how many floors would account for a thousand years, but with the uneven size of each storey it was difficult to tell.

"Maybe it'd be easiest to start at the bottom and work our way up," Tenzen suggested. "That way, you may be able to follow Daisuke's memories backwards."

"I never wanted to explore that man's thoughts in detail," Rakurai grumbled, but he followed Tenzen all the way to the bottom of the spiral stairs, moving by touch as the light grew dimmer. When he tilted his head back, faint light glimmered above him. Jumon's wisdom didn't brighten the floors of his archive, and maybe that was the point. If Tenzen was right, Jumon had wanted his archives to send wisdom into the world, not keep it within.

Inky darkness engulfed the base of the stairs, broken only by tiny flickers of light coming from the scroll-filled hall. Here and there, a light shone a little brighter, but most of the scrolls had no light of their own and some appeared to soak up what meagre glow there was in their vicinity.

"If I was in the least bit cynical," Rakurai mused, "I would look in the patches of darkness for Daisuke's memories."

Tenzen's eyebrows rose at the proclamation. "I never thought that he was evil," he said. "Vain, maybe. Misguided, perhaps. But mostly vain."

"You never thought much of the Yuvine to begin with, but you think more highly of Daisuke than I do."

"You've called him a snake, Rakurai. Snakes are not evil." He touched Rakurai's shoulder, a brush meant to comfort, and Rakurai allowed himself a moment to lean into the touch. "We could spend years here and never find what we seek," he sighed.

"So we could. But we'll never find anything if we don't search." Tenzen dropped a kiss to his temple in passing before he entered the dim hall. His fingertips brushed the seals on each scroll as he walked and Rakurai marvelled at the speed with which Tenzen absorbed their content. His mortal mind was not built that way and he had to read each memory at a much slower speed.

To make it easier on himself he chose only scrolls marked with the Yamakage seal, touching them with his fingertips when he found them. He let himself absorb the images emanating from the scrolls and tried not to judge what he saw. It was surprisingly arduous work.

He was two levels up from the lowest storey when he had a first glimpse of what he sought.

Gedele Perkhon, regal in a deep purple gown with silver lacing that had been fashionable two hundred years earlier, faced an annoyed Daisuke. The Yamakage elder sat seiza, back stiff as a board, and glared.

Gedele ignored Daisuke's anger. "Don't tell me that you never noticed the drop in power just after a new clan forms," she said, voice as measured as her countenance. "I was a child, half a world away and at the beginning of my training, when the Egyptian clan rose. Yet I felt the lessening of the powers available to us all. My mentor always likened it to butter being spread over too much bread."

Daisuke's sour face showed his disgust with the domestic comparison.

"Then the Sierra Leonian clan formed and magics that came easy now require more effort. My elder hunters report that their stamina is not what it used to be. You're the eldest living Yuvine, Daisuke. You must have noticed."

"Of course I did," Daisuke muttered.

Rakurai heard the lie. Whether due to lack of power or self-awareness, Daisuke had never felt the effects Gedele had described. Rakurai hadn't either, but he'd been born after the rise of the Sierra Leonian clan, and no new clans had formed since.

He turned the conversation over in his mind. Gedele Perkhon was the leader Yamakage Daisuke was not. She wouldn't just visit Daisuke to share an interesting nugget of information. She would have come seeking a solution, because the Yuvine slowly losing their powers *was* a problem.

He touched the scroll again and re-entered the memory.

"If the rise of new clans causes this power drain, then we must stop new clans from rising," Daisuke said as if all it took was his decree.

Gedele waited while Daisuke cudgelled his brain. "It always starts with the witches," she offered finally. "With witches and Yuvine who consort with witches and study their magic."

That was a threat Daisuke understood and could answer. "Then we monitor the clans for Yuvine who show such proclivities and prevent them from taking their studies too far."

A lump of ice formed in Rakurai's stomach. He yanked his fingers off the scroll. "Tenzen!"

CROSSING THE BRIDGE

"This could be what we're looking for," Tenzen said grimly, lifting his fingers from the scroll. "The Perkhon elder has no scruples. She's as ruthless as Jumon."

"Tenzen!"

"What? She's scared Daisuke silly with just a few words. He'll do anything now to stop new Yuvine clans from forming."

"Well, yes, but you said Gedele Perkhon is—"

"As ruthless as Jumon. You Yuvine have placed Jumon on a pedestal he doesn't belong on. He was obsessed with learning. He risked his life and the lives of his followers for facts. What is that if not ruthless?"

Rakurai swallowed his objections. All but one. "I've never heard that Gedele Perkhon pursued knowledge."

Tenzen touched the scroll again. Gedele's disdain for Daisuke's abilities was easy to read. She had a well-informed mind, but she didn't covet knowledge for knowledge's sake the way Jumon had done. For Gedele, knowledge was a weapon.

"Not like Jumon, no. That one wanted to *know* and he was mostly content with knowing. Gedele wants to know because it gives her an advantage. Can you tell how much she despises Daisuke? She considers him a weaponless fool."

"If knowledge is her weapon, then she's not wrong," Rakurai said.

"Agreed. He'd rather ferret out secrets he can hold over someone's head, so they do his bidding."

Rakurai turned into a slim, still column in the gloom of the hall. "What if that's why he keeps sending assassins after me? I refused to kill the Lugano hunters."

"You didn't know why he wanted Ricci and Alyssa Lugano out of the way."

"If I'd followed the order, I'd be complicit. I refused and now—"

"You're a liability. Someone who knows that he's killing Yuvine." Tenzen reached for Rakurai as if the only way to keep him safe was by keeping him close.

He rested his fingers on the scroll's seal, his mind on the two elders, but no new insights came to him.

"I must check on Raijin." Gone was Rakurai's assurance that Raijin was safe.

"Rakurai?"

"Until now, I only knew that the leader of my clan ordered me to kill two Yuvine hunters because they consorted with witches. And I thought it a ludicrous idea he made up to placate me. Now I know his real reason."

"What difference does it make?"

Rakurai's body drew taut. "Daisuke collects secrets, Tenzen. Secrets that the likes of his secretary and our younger cousins collect for him. And Raijin—"

"What about him?"

"He reads… about witchcraft." Rakurai's voice was soft in the darkness. Tenzen felt his reluctance to follow the thought to its conclusion. "He studied shamanism while learning about his gifts. But he also loves books, the older the better, and—"

"You're worried that Daisuke may find out." Tenzen went back to the scroll. "This matter of new clans rising is important to Gedele Perkhon. Daisuke seems only wishful to appear decisive. I'm not sure he even knew what she spoke of."

Rakurai calmed. His brows knitted as he thought. "That was my impression also. That he'd never experienced what she described." He looked up suddenly, and pinned Tenzen with his gaze. "Is it true? Does each new clan diminish the powers of the existing ones?"

"I don't know," Tenzen admitted. "Jumon brought celestial magic to the human realm and distributed it to his followers, who came together to form the Yamakage clan. A few generations later, one of your ancestors married a human shaman. They gathered likeminded people, and their son eventually founded the Perkhon clan. And no, I don't know how that's done. But if we assume that the celestial magic in the human realm is limited to that which Jumon brought with him…"

"Then Gedele might be right. More clans mean the magic is shared between more Yuvine."

"It's possible. Does it justify killing Yuvine and stopping the rise of new clans? I don't know."

"If two clan leaders join forces to kill other Yuvine… that might be a secret worth keeping."

"It makes Gedele Perkhon as much a threat to you as your elder. Maybe more so, since she's clearly the more ruthless of the two. Though I can't see her sending human assassins after you, either."

Rakurai sighed. "I don't know her well enough to judge that," he admitted. "But if she's worried enough about new clans to target any Yuvine with an interest in the arcane arts…"

He vacillated between wanting to explore further and wanting to head home to check on Raijin, and Tenzen pushed his own wants and wishes aside. He'd watched Raijin as he'd watched Rakurai and didn't want harm to come to either. "Let's go warn your son," he said, letting go of the scroll. "Now we've found a thread we can keep pulling on, we can come back another day to look for more."

Four rafeet stood on the far side of the bridge when Tenzen stepped out of the archives. He wasn't one to curse, but he very much felt the need to do so in that moment.

Rakurai wasn't as restrained. "Is there really no way to open the veil on this side of the bridge?"

"No. But the rafeet can't breech the wards. Nor do they want to die, so they won't venture onto the bridge to fight us in the fog."

"So they'll wait until we reach the other side. How does that help us?"

"It helps because the wards lessen once we cross the halfway point. Let me go first and drive them back to give us level terrain to fight."

"I don't like that idea. You're only just healed."

"Do you have a better one?"

"No."

"Well, then…" He stepped onto the bridge, and mist curled out of the chasm. Three steps later, the fog closed around him. The vague, featureless glow wreaked havoc on his senses, and Tenzen kept one hand on the guide rope. He'd heard stories of men losing their balance on the narrow bridge, their screams echoing long after their bodies had hit the roiling waters below.

He manifested the whip he'd fashioned after Rakurai had gifted him the lightning and held it, ready-charged. The bridge swayed when Rakurai stepped onto the ropes, and he braced himself to ride out the undulation.

A particularly heavy gust yanked his feet from under him. Tenzen scrabbled for purchase, the soles of his boots sliding on damp hemp. He smashed into the guide rope, clutching at it with desperate strength while it stretched under his weight until he hung suspended over the abyss, not daring to move an inch.

Tenzen!

Shocks rippled through the ropes as Rakurai fought to balance the flimsy bridge.

Still here. Just.

What the fuck are you doing?

Trying not to let go. Hands on the guide rope, feet on the bridge, body stretched long over nothing... Tenzen had been in more comfortable positions. *Brace yourself.*

Whatever Rakurai did steadied the bridge. The guide ropes stiffened, and the bridge's rocking gentled to a sway. Trapped between two moving ropes, Tenzen clenched every muscle and fought to right himself. Slowly. Without setting the bridge to rocking once more.

Sweat dripped off him when his head and feet were both in line and vertical. His fingers ached from his desperate clutch at the rope. *And in all that... I didn't drop the whip*, he said, incredulous.

As if it would have done you any good had you gone into the ravine. Don't do that!

Forgive me. Tenzen allowed himself a couple of deep breaths, then set foot in front of foot, moving as if over eggshells. The gusts eased a fraction while the mist grew thicker. And all Tenzen's senses waited for a touch like the lightest gossamer.

It came long after he thought he'd passed the middle of the bridge, but it came.

The fog lightened in tiny increments even as the gusts strengthened once more. With his nerves still twanging from the near-miss, Tenzen fought for balance. *Someone wants us off this bridge.*

It certainly feels like it. How far along are you?

Over the middle. And... Tenzen squinted at the shapes in the opaque white haze. *I can see them,* he informed Rakurai. *Clustering at the head of the bridge.*

Give them my regards.

Tenzen swung the whip in a wide arc. The lightning-charged cord left a vapour trail, allowing him to see the swish to the left, and the answering flick to the right. A scream answered the move. Tenzen swung again and again, awkward and graceless, while he clung to the guide rope with his left hand and tiptoed to the end of the bridge as fast as he dared.

Move left when you step off the bridge, Rakurai said suddenly.

The mist disappeared as if he'd passed through a curtain, and Tenzen chanced a couple of long, loping strides. His leading foot hit solid ground. *I'm off the bridge!*

I'm right behind you.

Two of the waiting rafeet sported lightning burns. It didn't slow them down. Just made them madder. All four rushed him the moment he was clear of the wards, leaving him little time for anything but whip and sword to defend himself.

They're fighting as a unit, he warned Rakurai. It was a technique the rafeet had adopted over the last few years, and they were all the deadlier for it.

Rakurai's whip shot past him, snatching one of the rafeet from the fight and dropping it over the edge of the cliff into the sea. It screamed horribly as it fell and the remaining rafeet hesitated for a fraction of a heartbeat.

It was all the gap Rakurai needed to join Tenzen on level ground. He wielded two lightning-charged whips with stunning dexterity, separating the rafeet and creating space for Tenzen's attacks.

They moved in a well-choreographed dance, with lightning crackling and flashing around them as if they fought in a thunderstorm.

Tenzen killed two rafeet in quick succession.

Rakurai decapitated the third one with a vicious slash of his whip.

The absence of screams was their reward, and as the bridge's wards grew dormant, the gusty wind became a soft breeze. Two steps brought Tenzen to Rakurai's side and they kissed right there, on the headland, with three dead rafeet beside them.

"Go, before I can't bear to let you out of my sight." Tenzen opened a path into Rakurai's garden.

Rakurai smiled at the view but didn't step through the veil. Instead, he wrapped his arms around Tenzen's neck and kissed him again. Sweetly this time, until neither had breath left. "Talk to me," he requested. "I've missed hearing your voice in my mind these last weeks in the human realm. I'd not realised how much of a comfort it is to me."

Tenzen touched the back of his hand to Rakurai's cheek. Then he trailed two fingers over the obsidian pendant at Rakurai's throat. "Keep this close."

"Always." Rakurai turned and stepped through the veil, leaving Tenzen behind.

Tenzen stared at the empty air, craving Rakurai's return. He'd hoped to spend more time with Rakurai, but they couldn't discount what they'd learned.

Daisuke and Gedele had a secret that threatened any Yuvine with an interest in witchcraft. A secret that might threaten Raijin. And Rakurai would have died in the inn had Tenzen not been there.

Tenzen couldn't ignore the signs of danger. He also couldn't let himself be caught in the human realm again. Not like he had been, visible to humans, and without his powers. He'd be no use to Rakurai that way.

Keep my shrine near you at all times, he whispered across two worlds.

The chuckle he received in reply eased his worry. *Raijin is safe. I'll talk to him about his books. And I'll carry stones from my garden from now on.*

Thank you. Tenzen breathed out.

They'd both learned that lesson. Now Rakurai would make sure that Tenzen had legitimate access to the human realm. It would not be pleasant, because the desecration of a Shinigami's shrine triggered a special kind of rage. But Tenzen would never mistake Rakurai for an enemy, even in a rage. He was sure of that.

Alone as he hadn't been in weeks, he gathered the souls of the slain demons. Another four souls who had been reborn in the darkness beyond the worlds. Four new chances to unravel that mystery. He tucked them away, safe until he could release them in his garden.

Right now, he needed to learn more of Gedele's plans. How many Yuvine had she and Daisuke killed to prevent new clans? How did she choose her victims? And was there any danger to Rakurai and Raijin?

I'm returning to the archive, he told Rakurai. *I'll be able to hear you but coming to your aid won't be so easy. Plan accordingly.*

I'm planning on nothing more strenuous than sharing dinner with my son. I'll not leave the manor and the place is well warded.

Tenzen took it as the reassurance it was and, with only the slightest hesitation, headed back towards the rope bridge and the archive that lay beyond.

HOMECOMING

"Father!" Raijin's wide-eyed stare made Rakurai wish he'd taken the time to make himself presentable. A quick downward glance confirmed that the mist on the bridge had turned the dust from the archives into a sticky goo that clung to him in streaks and smears.

"I'm not hurt. Just travel-stained and weary," he answered the question Raijin hadn't asked.

"You didn't say you were travelling to the Otherworld."

"I didn't know I'd be crossing the veil," he admitted. "I should be home for a while now."

Raijin brightened. "Would you like tea?" A delicate blush stained his cheeks, and when Rakurai followed his gaze, he saw a tea table, brazier, and cushion set out on the corner of the engawa overlooking the garden.

"You finished your work for the day, I see," he teased. "Let me change out of these dirty clothes and then I'll join you gladly."

Raijin has grown up too fast, he told Tenzen as he washed archive dust off his hands and face.

Why do you sound as if this fact displeases you?

It doesn't displease me. I mourn the time we've lost. All the days and weeks I haven't spent with him.

There is little value in mourning that which you can't change, Tenzen said.

He was right. But the feeling of time running out nagged at Rakurai. The conversation between Daisuke and Gedele had spawned a cloud of dread that grew larger every time he considered the circumstances. If he let it grow unchecked, it would soon blot out his ability to reason.

Gedele said it always starts with witches. We should find out whether Ricci and Alyssa Lugano studied witchcraft, he said. *Which won't be easy in that mess of an archive. Curses!*

Tenzen didn't sound in the least put out. *I'll see what I can find.*

We don't even know what we're looking for.

Leave it to me. Tenzen's tone was soothing. *You can trust me, Rakurai.*

I know I can. Rakurai wanted to apologise, but his thoughts were so tangled, he didn't know where to begin.

What is it you fear?

Good question. Rakurai thought about it. Unspecified threats were hard to defend against. All they did was ramp up his worries. *I'm afraid we'll find proof that Gedele and Daisuke are conspiring to kill Yuvine. And that Daisuke finds out about Raijin's reading choices and targets him,* he admitted in the end.

Raijin heads to the Custodia in a few months' time. That should remove him from Daisuke's orbit, no?

You're right, Rakurai sighed. *I'm no doubt fretting over nothing.*

Not nothing. But more than we understand right now. I fear that Gedele and Daisuke are interfering in something that should have been left alone.

I don't understand.

Neither do I. Not yet. But Jumon was… almost a force of nature. He made a bargain with the Unseen Power. If the decisions of your elders were to nix that bargain—

You're afraid.

Terrified.

There was not an ounce of humour in Tenzen's deep voice. He meant every word. And if a death god was terrified… *How can I help?*

Watch your back while I try and learn what's going on. Spend time with your son and enjoy it.

I will.

Say it as if you believe it. Haven't we learned to make the most of the time we have?

I'm caught between desires as I'm caught between worlds, Rakurai admitted. *When I'm with you, I mourn the time I'm not spending with Raijin. Yet when I'm here I regret that I'm losing out on being with you.*

Tenzen was silent for a long time. When he spoke, his mental voice was soft and hesitant. *You've never said that before.*

I know. I'm sorry if I gave you the impression that you don't matter. If I let you believe that I only cared for Raijin. I'm a greedy bastard who wants to spend time with you both.

Don't say that. You prove that you care for me every time you come to my aid, and never so much as in these last few weeks. Don't spoil the time you have with either one of us with feelings of guilt.

That was easier said than done, Rakurai realised when he joined Raijin on the veranda. His son had not just added a second cushion, stirred the brazier to life, and replenished the tea set. He'd been to the kitchens, too, and a tray of Rakurai's favourite dishes sat ready on one corner of the table.

"You make an excellent host," he said as he settled on his cushion.

Raijin flushed. "I've been trying to uphold your honour, when… when you weren't here."

Rakurai wanted to apologise, but he had no idea where to begin. He was doing his duty, not wasting time wandering the lands like a ronin. Only… he *had* spent the last weeks watching over Tenzen as he recovered. And since meeting Tenzen he'd often lingered for a few extra days in his realm. But he could be here right now.

"You've done us proud," he said, picking a piece of grilled eel from its dish and popping it into his mouth. The savoury taste of the sweet-salty glaze almost made him moan. "Are you forced to entertain many visitors while I'm gone? I've never been comfortable leaving you alone."

"I know. You've told me so before. And I do understand about duty and..." Raijin twirled his chopsticks. A habit Rakurai had always found endearing, while Naomi had tried to break Raijin of it for years. "May I ask you something?"

"Of course."

"Do you really have a lover in the Otherworld?"

Did you hear that? Rakurai wanted nothing so much as the death god opening the veil and joining them for tea, but Tenzen didn't reply. *Tenzen?*

More silence, which probably meant that the wards around the archive stopped Tenzen from hearing him. Rakurai turned his attention back to his son. Raijin was now as tall as he was, slender and swift, with the same dark eyes and pale hair that marked their line of the Yamakage. He was brave, too, asking questions Rakurai wouldn't have dared voice at his age.

"I suppose there are rumours?" he asked mildly.

"Plenty. Most are ridiculous. Or malicious." Raijin shrugged, trying to portray a lack of concern he didn't feel.

"Succubus, incubus, demon, creature with tentacles?"

"Among others. But rumours aside... is it true?"

"It is. He saved my life. More than once."

Raijin's eyes widened a little, whether at Rakurai's choice of lover or his answering so readily, Rakurai didn't know. They weren't in the habit of discussing such things. But Raijin was grown now.

Rakurai hid a smile behind another bite of grilled eel. Raijin's question had been a challenge. One he hadn't expected to be answered.

"Elder Daisuke came to visit me while you were gone," Raijin confided.

"He isn't one to miss an opportunity. Though he'd never have come if he didn't think you ready to accept responsibilities of your own."

Raijin's flush held both pleasure and embarrassment. "He came to talk about my service in the Custodia," he admitted.

Rakurai swallowed a snarl. He'd trained Raijin, had prepared him to serve as a hunter. But to have Daisuke barge in before Raijin had made his choice… "Of course, he did. Raijin, I know we talked about you serving in the Custodia. And yes, our branch of the Yamakage has always provided the clan's hunters. That doesn't mean it's your only option. If you'd like to—"

"No. I… I've always wanted to be a hunter. I prefer it to—" Raijin bit his lip. "Elder Daisuke. He… Father, he doesn't like you."

"He most definitely does not. He wants his orders to be followed without question, and I've always made my own choices." Rakurai wrapped an arm around his son's shoulders. "Your mother and I have tried to keep you away from clan politics to give you a chance to form your own opinions. I'm sorry if my actions affected your training."

Charcoal smoke rose in delicate curls from the brazier. The kettle hummed and Raijin turned his attention to the task of making tea. Rakurai didn't interrupt. He cherished each conversation and silence they shared, as much as he wished that Tenzen and Raijin could meet. Maybe now that Raijin was of age...

"I do want to serve as a hunter," Raijin said after he'd handed Rakurai a fresh cup of tea. "From what you've told me, the Custodia seems a good starting point. I'd be fulfilling my duty to our clan while staying away from Elder Daisuke's... court." He spoke the last words with a little curl to his lip.

"You no longer care for your cousins?"

"Have you seen what's become of them?" Raijin straightened. "It's as you said. Elder Daisuke demands blind obedience, and that's what they're giving him. You've never... You always encouraged me to think and question, and I don't want to change."

"I'm glad to hear it." Rakurai didn't hide his pride. "The Custodia may yet gain greater importance. Beyond being a proving ground for clan hunters, I mean. The rafeet have begun to fight in co-ordinated groups. We don't know how they've learned to do so, nor where they've found the power. It's possible they're a new kind of rafeet. They're certainly a stronger breed. But if this trend continues, single hunters may not be enough to stop them."

"What about the rafeet who used its spawn to weave a net? Is it one of the new kind?" Raijin sat, teacup forgotten in his fingers, waiting for an answer.

"That would be my guess."

"You killed that one."

"Yes, but not alone." It had taken him and Tenzen wielding lightning to destroy the rafeet's body. Rakurai remembered lashing the dead demon's heart with lightning over and over before it finally yielded and crumbled to dust. It had taken so much more effort... "Even separated from its spawn it was hard to kill and—"

The crunch of gravel preceded the hollow tap of sandals on wooden steps. Rakurai's steward appeared around the corner. He bowed, face expressionless and hands hidden in the sleeves of his kimono, but Rakurai had known him too long not to read his regret at having to interrupt his and Raijin's time together. "What is it?"

"A messenger arrived from the Custodia. He says his message is urgent."

CALL FOR HELP

A scream of rage wrecked the peace in Tenzen's garden. He'd come here straight from the archive, seeking reassurance and a quiet place to consider what he'd found. But the scream couldn't be ignored.

Tenzen reached for his weapons. His next step brought him to a small plateau that overlooked a steeply terraced hillside and the valley beyond. Everything here was lush and green. Flowers bloomed and butterflies tumbled and wheeled between them. Serenity ruled as far as he could see.

The sounds of battle all came from behind him.

He spun, whip in one hand and soul sword in the other and found Okandi challenging six rafeet and a posse of smaller demons. The eldest Shinigami was a tiny woman—her head barely reached Tenzen's chin—but she was fierce and fearless.

As Tenzen closed the distance between them, she dispatched one rafeet and squared off against the others.

Krull, hyeshi, and winged demons Tenzen hadn't seen since his youth darted down again and again, trying to pass the invisible line she defended.

She threw them a look of pure loathing.

Tenzen didn't need an invitation to join the fight. His whip snaked out, laden with lightning, and swiped three of the demons from the air in a single snap.

One of the rafeet howled.

It sounded like a warning and the posse of small demons scattered.

Invisible, sticky tendrils caught on Tenzen's hair and clothes as they passed him, and he realised with a jolt that they wielded a net like the one that had trapped him.

He darted across the plateau, boots squishing through blood and viscera, until he stood beside Okandi. They weren't friends. They hadn't met or spoken since the world was young. But she had called for help, and he had answered the call.

"Watch the red one," he told her, readying the whip once more. "He weaves the powers of the smaller demons into a net to encircle us."

She nodded grimly and turned her back to his, giving each of them room to fight. The winged demons regrouped out of reach of Tenzen's whip. The rafeet were not so cautious, darting close to rake at them with their curved claws.

Tenzen held them at bay. Over and over his whip snapped out, opening long slashes on the demons' bodies. Lightning sizzled. The air stank of metal, grease, and burning flesh. And the demons' screams of pain and fury echoed around the plateau.

Tenzen's whip held enough lightning to injure the attacking demons. It wasn't strong enough to kill them. Once the red rafeet realised it, the net began to close once more.

Okandi skewered another rafeet on her long, straight blade and used the shorter sword in her other hand to cut off its head. They needed to cut out its heart to kill it properly, but that could wait until they'd defeated the other demons.

Especially the red rafeet.

Tenzen remembered the feel of the net drawing tighter the more he struggled against it. He had no wish to spend another eighteen years as a demon's captive.

He hacked and slashed at the rafeet coming at him, a whirl of sword and whip. A horizontal slash took the nearest rafeet's head. It rolled away while the body crumpled, coming to rest against an unseen barrier.

The net.

Closer than it had been before. Almost surrounding him and Okandi.

He slashed the whip through the sticky tendrils and used the backward swing to swipe a group of krull from the air.

It wasn't enough.

The net reformed.

Drew closer.

And the atmosphere on the plateau suddenly grew thick and stale.

Okandi gasped. Tenzen, too, struggled for breath, sucking air with his mouth wide open. The light dimmed, and the screams of the demons came to him from far away. He swayed, focussed on staying upright, and the dull thud of his sword hitting the turf jolted him back to alertness. He was a hairsbreadth from passing out and he needed… He needed…

He let the whip fall from his fingers, raised both hands, and imagined he was Rakurai.

Power rushed through him and lightning, so bright his eyes watered, bloomed in his palms. He sent it forth and the bolts hit the rafeet, turning it into a ball of white light. When the brightness faded, two shrivelled, blackened feet were all that remained of the demon.

Okandi recovered first from the shock.

"Impressive," she huffed, and decapitated the remaining demon with a single slash of her sword.

"Useful." Tenzen shook off his stupor and climbed to his feet. His body protested each move as if he'd taken a vicious beating. He'd never been able to use Rakurai's gift this way and he hadn't expected it to work.

Maybe he'd been due a touch of good fortune.

He found the nearest rafeet, sliced open its chest and extracted the heart. That brought back memories of Rakurai beside a lake, incinerating the heart of a demon with lashes of his whip.

It felt like an awfully long time ago.

He dropped the heart onto the rafeet's body, held out his hand and created another ball of lightning. This one charred the grass and Tenzen winced at the sight.

"A new plaything?"

Tenzen felt heat burn his cheeks. "Too much for what's needed, I dare say. But it will serve."

She didn't argue, and between them they ensured that the rafeet stayed dead and that none of the minor demons the rafeet had enslaved would live on as mindless walking corpses.

Soot, grime, and all manner of disgusting fluids stained their robes, but they smiled at each other when they lowered their weapons.

"Visit a while," Okandi invited. "You can wash off the stench of battle. There's food and tea. And I've not seen you in far too long."

Even as a young Shinigami, Tenzen had preferred his solitude. He hadn't mingled with the other Shinigami, nor with the humans that inhabited the Otherworld or any of its creatures. Meeting Rakurai had reminded him of the pleasure to be had in company. Now that he'd come to Okandi's aid when she called, it would be rude to turn down her invitation.

"Thank you," he said. "I would like that very much."

"You've made this whole valley your garden?" Tenzen gazed at the flights of terraces that turned steep hillsides into level ground for planting. Tea bushes grew on the strips of land, along with rice, corn, and bright flowers. Busy and well-tended, the hill resembled a miniature city, guarded by a tiny woman dressed in white and populated by butterflies.

"My garden has always been here." She gazed fondly at the view. "It doesn't change as yours is said to do and, over the years, I've arranged it to my liking."

"Your garden doesn't change? Ever?" Tenzen couldn't imagine knowing his garden's every secret.

"It has no need to do so. The souls I care for are sure of their path either side of their existence here. They're not, like yours, in need of guidance and self-discovery. How do you handle all the myriads of demands they make on you?"

Tenzen blinked. He'd never considered his souls demanding, nor had he wished for another task.

Okandi didn't press him for an answer. She smiled and held out a cup of tea for him to take. "That tea grew twenty feet from here." She gestured at the uppermost terrace. "And it's all the better for it. I will fill you a bag to take with you when you leave."

"You do not owe me—"

"I know. It isn't payment. Even though I called and you came, it wasn't—" Embarrassment tinged her cheeks as if asking for help was somehow shameful. "I screamed my anger."

"I know. I heard. It pains me to see that the attacks have increased in your part of the Otherworld as well."

"Your garden is under threat?"

"More than ever before. The protections grow thin, and all manner of demons now breach the defences."

"And the Yuvine have forsaken their duty." Okandi spoke the same words he had levelled at Rakurai when they'd first met.

"Not all of them. There's a hunter I could have called to help us," he admitted. "But he's only just returned to his home, and I wanted to see what we faced before I asked for his aid."

"I heard that you'd brought a Yuvine to your garden. I didn't want to believe it."

"It's true." Tenzen smiled. "I was returning from the human realm when a rafeet trapped me in its net. It held me captive for eighteen years, until Rakurai happened past my prison on his hunt and helped me escape."

"He differs from the Yuvine I have met, then."

"He differs from the ones I've met, too. Four hunters passed my prison in those eighteen years. And none of them could bestir themselves to help. Yamakage Rakurai isn't like the others. He fights to hold back the darkness as is written in the agreement. If I'd called him today, he would have come to our aid." Even if it would have cost him precious time with his son.

She set down her cup without a comment and gazed across her hillside and the valley beyond. "We are spread too thin," she said finally. "We always were. But before

Jumon, our strength was enough. Now the Yuvine are failing in their duties and the magic building up in the human realm…." A bunch of shrivelled leaves appeared in her palm, brown and crackling. "It poisons the earth."

"What does?"

"The Yuvine became the balance between our worlds, remember?"

Tenzen had heard that said after Jumon had come to the Otherworld and made the agreement. That in exchange for the gift of celestial magic the Yuvine would balance the worlds and help them hold back the darkness. It had never made much sense. But Okandi was the eldest of the Shinigami. Her talents bound her to the earth and Tenzen saw no reason to doubt her.

"Every living thing grows and dies, Tenzen. Jumon created the Yuvine by sharing the celestial magic he'd brought to the human realm. I always expected that the Yuvine, having been human, would eventually succumb to human vices and squander Jumon's gift. That is the way of birth and death and rebirth." She sighed. "Our worlds are due for change. But nobody ever wants to live through those changes when they happen."

Her words sent a jolt through Tenzen's mind. He'd seen a record of that birth, death and rebirth when he'd stood with Rakurai in the Yuvine archive. Seen it, without really seeing it. He was sure of it. "Explain it to me."

"Jumon promised that the Yuvine would help keep back the darkness. We took that to mean that Yuvine hunters will join us in defending the two worlds. But fighting is only part of the agreement, and I'm not sure the Yuvine properly understand the matter."

"They're not the only ones," Tenzen grumbled.

"You rehabilitate souls, Tenzen. When would you have had time to ponder Jumon's agreement with the Unseen Power?"

"Maybe I should have made time. You did."

"My tasks differ from yours," she disagreed. "As for Jumon's bargain… The balance lies in the exchange of magics. Jumon brought celestial magic to the human realm, creating a shortage in one realm and an excess in the other. Every Yuvine who crosses the veil brings earthbound magic to the Otherworld. It's this magic that strengthens our defences."

Tenzen closed his eyes. He remembered years when he'd spent more time outside his garden, fighting, than he'd spent inside tending the souls in his care, and times when demon threats had been few and far between. Birth, death, and rebirth—Okandi had reminded him— were the mainstays of life.

He recalled the conversation of Gedele Perkhon and Yamakage Daisuke that had made him so uneasy, and the discussion between Gedele Perkhon and Custodia Commander Tan Hao that had sent him to his garden to think.

His mind merged darkness, pinpricks of light, and the swirl of stairs heading deep into a cliff until his heart beat up a storm and cold sweat covered his upper lip and hairline. "Have you explored the Yuvine archive?" he asked, opening his eyes again.

Okandi shook her head. "I've never seen the need."

"You should at least visit. There's no need to bother yourself with the records, just go to the lowest level and look up."

Okandi's violet eyes glinted as she studied him. Tenzen felt as if she were reading his thoughts, and the very idea made him uncomfortable. Then she held out her hand. On her palm lay a spiral shell, a symmetrical swirl that grew from a tiny casing that had protected a newly born snail, to whorls that were large enough to hold the fully grown animal. "You're telling me that this is not what I will see."

Tenzen shook his head. "No. Not even close. The pattern is uneven. Like a burst of growth, then a slow decline until there's another burst." He shook his head again, pictured the spiral stairs and the mix of tall, deep halls and low-ceilinged shallow ones. There had been symmetry in the unevenness until… "Now the pattern has come to a halt. Because the Yuvine are interfering in the natural order." He told her what he'd learned.

"As it was foretold." Okandi breathed out. "We must find a way to strengthen our defences, or both our worlds will be lost to the darkness."

Tenzen drained his cup, the tea suddenly bitter in his mouth. "I wonder what powers we'll need to do that."

Okandi did not smile. "I can't see the future any more than you. If we had that talent, we could have called the Yuvine to task long before they grew negligent."

"Or reminded ourselves not to hand over part of our duties to the Yuvine."

"Also true. We're complicit in the situation. Speak to your Yuvine while I try to learn what went wrong. Maybe we can devise a way that will not end with the destruction of everything we hold dear."

RESISTING THE DARKNESS

The Custodia's messenger had departed as promptly as he'd arrived, leaving Rakurai sitting beside the tea set contemplating yet another journey he had no wish to undertake.

Did you hear that? Tenzen?

Tenzen didn't reply and a tendril of worry snaked through Rakurai's mind. Tenzen had promised he'd be able to hear Rakurai while he explored the archive. Had something happened?

"Let me come with you," Raijin begged, snapping Rakurai back to the present.

"It's a council meeting, Raijin. Hours of speeches." *Laced with lies, blackmail, and bribery.* Rakurai swallowed the words. Neither Naomi nor he had cared for politics, but Raijin might find one day that he had a taste for it. Rakurai should leave him to make his own choices and not poison his mind.

"The council meeting won't take all your time, and maybe we could—"

"No." Rakurai wanted nothing more than work beside Raijin, but he couldn't allow himself that indulgence. "The message said nothing about why we were summoned. While I think you're ready to serve in the Custodia, I don't want to risk dropping you in the middle of a battle."

"You think there'll be a battle?"

"I don't know. The council called for all designated hunters, and demon attacks have been on the rise. It's possible they'll send us out in a group."

"That's...."

"Uncommon. Which is why I'd prefer it if you stayed here. Start your tenure with the Custodia in the new year." He settled his palm on Raijin's shoulder. "We'll get the chance to hunt together. I promise."

Raijin didn't argue, but he drooped in disappointment under Rakurai's touch. Rakurai wanted to hug him.

"When will you leave?"

"As soon as I've gathered my gear." The words emerged slowly and sank like stones. He'd not even been home for a day. "Be safe."

Rakurai expected Raijin to turn on his heel and walk away. It was his way of keeping face, and Rakurai had never chided him for it. But Raijin chose a different path this time. He threw his arms around Rakurai, hugging him tight.

"Watch your back," he whispered, just loud enough for Rakurai to hear. "I want that chance to hunt by your side."

Rakurai hugged him back, the lump in his throat almost too big to breathe through. "I promise."

Tenzen! Are you safe?

I'm safe.

You didn't answer me.

Rakurai sagged with relief when the veil opened in the middle of the room and showed him Tenzen sitting on the veranda of his house with not a fold of his robe or a lock of hair out of place. His eyes were a different matter, though. They blazed with an emotion Rakurai couldn't decipher. He thought he saw rage but also self-loathing and guilt, and none of these made sense.

"I'm sorry if I worried you. I can't hear you while I'm in another Shinigami's garden." He studied the pack in Rakurai's hand. "You were planning to spend time with Raijin. What has happened?"

Rakurai forced himself to step through the veil without looking back. It was early afternoon in the Otherworld, the sun warm on the smooth boards of Tenzen's veranda. "All hunters serving in the Custodia have been summoned to attend the Solstice Council."

"I thought you'd left the Custodia to train Raijin."

"It's more in the way of a temporary arrangement," Rakurai said. He dropped his pack and then leaned his back against the balustrade, watching Tenzen. "After Naomi died, Daisuke agreed that it was in the clan's best interest for me to oversee Raijin's training. He sent one of his more troublesome nephews to the Custodia in my place. Officially, though, I'm still the designated hunter for the Yamakage clan. Which is why they sent for me, I assume."

Tenzen studied the folds of his robe as if they revealed the secrets of the universe. "Did Tan Hao call this meeting?"

"Yes. Tenzen, what is this about? What's wrong?"

"You shouldn't go."

"Excuse me?"

"A council meeting would be an excellent opportunity to get rid of you, don't you think?"

"Tan Hao wouldn't let himself be used in this way," Rakurai disagreed. "That'd be outright murder."

"And Daisuke asking you to kill Ricci and Alyssa Lugano was different?"

Rakurai breathed out and let his shoulders slump. There was no need for posturing between them. "Tenzen talk to me. What makes you say this? Something you found in the archives?"

"Something I found… yes." Tenzen sat like a statue.

The hair on the nape of Rakurai's neck stood straight up. "Tenzen? What is it? What did you find?"

"Do you remember the way the archive rooms burrowed into the cliff? How there were high, spacious halls reaching deep into the rock, and shallow ones with a roof so low we could barely stand upright?"

"Yes."

"From the lighthouse on down, the halls form a pattern. A tall, deep hall starts the cycle. Then, with every turn of the stairs, the halls get shallower and lower, each holding fewer thoughts and memories than the layer above. Until there's another huge hall, followed by halls that get smaller as time passes."

"And?"

"There are ten of the huge halls."

He stopped there, and Rakurai waited for more. When it became clear that Tenzen wasn't going to say anything else, he crossed the veranda and sat beside his lover. "I don't understand."

Tenzen looked up, then, and his eyes hadn't lost their troubled expression. "The archive holds twelve thousand years of memories, from the early Yamakage clan in the lighthouse itself all the way down to the present day. I think that the huge halls form whenever a new Yuvine clan rises. Because the members of each new clan experience their gifts and the Otherworld for the first time, there's an influx of new memories and ideas. Over time, their enthusiasm dwindles. They stop exploring the two worlds as the Yuvine before them have done, and the halls holding memories grow smaller. Until the next clan rises and the cycle repeats."

He fell silent, and Rakurai closed his eyes and pictured the archive. "It's regular. A repeating pattern," he realised. "But right at the end, the pattern... stops. There are more shallow, low-ceilinged halls than there should be."

"Correct. Okandi, the eldest of my kind, called the archive a representation of birth, growth, death, and rebirth. And maybe it was that until Gedele Perkhon and your elder decided to stop the rise of new Yuvine clans. I don't know what it represents now."

"Failure."

"Maybe."

Rakurai reached for Tenzen's hand and twined their fingers. "I want to help," he said. "Please tell me what's bothering you."

"Is an interruption to the cycle of birth and rebirth not enough?"

"It's plenty. But it isn't what bothers you most. It's just what you use to distract yourself. So please, tell me."

"You won't like it."

"Tell me anyway."

Tenzen's fingers closed tightly around Rakurai's. "I returned to the archive to find out how many Yuvine Gedele and your elder had killed in their attempt to stop new clans. I... there must be a reason other than preserving the power of the existing Yuvine. Especially since most Yuvine barely use their gifts." He broke off again.

"How many?"

"I don't know. Not yet. But I learned that, after you refused to kill the Luganos, Gedele Perkhon ordered Commander Tan Hao to deal with the problem, because Vigdis wasn't available."

A sudden punch in the gut couldn't have surprised Rakurai more than those words. "Tan Hao?"

"I know how highly you think of him. That's why I didn't want to tell you."

Shinigami didn't lie. Rakurai knew this, but he still searched for reasons that Tenzen was wrong. "Tan Hao officiated at my and Naomi's bonding ceremony. He's never been anything but honest and upright. I can't imagine he kills Yuvine on Gedele's orders."

"You struggled to believe that your own clan elder would give you such an order," Tenzen remarked. He poured wine for them both and handed a cup to Rakurai. "You don't seem to have the same problem when it comes to Vigdis Perkhon."

"Vigdis does whatever Gedele tells him to. He doesn't take orders from anyone else."

"But he serves in the Custodia?"

"Nominally." Rakurai chuckled and drained his glass. "Seems we're more alike than I thought."

"You're nothing alike. And distraction won't work for either one of us today. I'm worried, Rakurai. This last attempt on your life was more serious than all the others put together, and now Tan Hao calls you to a council meeting?"

Rakurai held out his cup for a refill. "I can defend myself. But do you realise that I'm about to send Raijin to serve in the Custodia?"

"Give him some credit, Rakurai. Your son can defend himself just as comprehensively. All he lacks is your experience."

They sat in silence for a time, gazing out over the rocks, moss, and gravel of Tenzen's formal garden. Rakurai knew the arrangement by heart, but today it didn't bring him any peace. They had too much to consider.

"I've never heard you mention another death god before," he said finally.

"Okandi. I went to help her defend her garden against a posse of rafeet. One of those could control smaller demons the way the rafeet that caught me controlled its human servants."

"Another one!"

"Quite. I feel as if I've walked the world blindfold," Tenzen admitted. "Wilfully so. Now the blindfold is gone, I see all my shortcomings and omissions."

Rakurai knew how that felt. He could have seen much more of Raijin's days if he'd made use of Tenzen's gifts. More than once Tenzen had offered to show him the past... and Rakurai had backed away every single time. His mind couldn't grasp the process, so he'd closed himself to the possibility. "Self-realisation is never painless. Tell me what you've learned."

"Okandi thinks that the veil, our defence against the darkness, is weakening, because Gedele Perkhon and your clan elder decided to stop the formation of new Yuvine clans."

"That makes no sense. If forming a new clan dilutes the power of all existing Yuvine, then how can having more clans help keep back the darkness?"

"Because the magic between our two worlds is a balance. Jumon took celestial magic to the human realm, brought you longevity, special gifts, and the ability to pass between the worlds."

"And in exchange, the Yuvine agreed to help defend the Otherworld."

"True, but there's more to it than fighting. According to Okandi, every Yuvine crossing the veil brings earthbound magic in their wake. Over time, as the existing Yuvine focussed on human realm concerns, that stream of earthbound magic would slow. Before it could stop and cause trouble a new clan would form, and Yuvine would visit the Otherworld again."

"And now, Gedele and Daisuke have made that impossible." Rakurai could see the logic. "I've never sensed or heard of earthbound magic. What does it do?"

"Toughen the veil and help protect our worlds, or so Okandi says. And since all of us have neglected our duties..."

"Neglected your duties? I've rarely seen anyone work harder than you do. How could you possibly neglect your duties?"

Tenzen refilled their cups. "Before Jumon, it was the task of the death gods to care for the souls that passed through the Otherworld and to defend our realm. After Jumon we focussed on souls rather than defence except when our gardens were threatened directly. We grew complacent because we had the Yuvine."

"Until we slackened in our duties, too," Rakurai finished, finally seeing the pattern.

"Yes. And now the defences allow all manner of demons into our worlds and the Yuvine are killing each other."

Rakurai curved his palm to Tenzen's cheek, hoping to erase the defeated, disgusted expression from Tenzen's face. He'd divided his time between Raijin and Tenzen, but who'd most needed his support? Tenzen had never asked anything of him, and Rakurai had always come down on the side of his young son. Now the bleakness in Tenzen's eyes made him wonder if that choice had been wise.

"I'll join you in that fight," he promised. "I'll take your information to the Solstice Council. Warn them of the increased attacks, remind them of our sworn duty."

"It will hardly endear you to the Council of Elders."

"Maybe not. But more than just the Council of Elders will hear my words. Some of them may join us."

Tenzen tightened his fingers on Rakurai's and leaned into his palm. "You're young," he said affectionately. "And so very optimistic."

It wasn't optimism, Tenzen realised when Rakurai bent to kiss him with single-minded focus. It was determination and the need to bend circumstances to his will.

When he was like this, Rakurai resembled his ancestor. Jumon had bargained with the Unseen Power though it could have cost him his life. And now Rakurai was ready to confront the Yuvine council and Tenzen did not want to let him do it alone.

A touch on his cheek tore him from his thoughts. Rakurai had been speaking to him. He covered Rakurai's fingers with his and held tight. "Forgive me. I was…"

"Distracted," Rakurai supplied with a tiny smile. "What happened to the serene death god I met in the rafeet's manor?"

Tenzen opened his mouth to answer, but Rakurai was faster. "That was a rhetorical question. The more I learn about all this, the more distracted I feel myself. How could we have misinterpreted Jumon's rules so disastrously?"

"Let's not worry about that tonight. It's not a problem the two of us can solve, and you'd be better off sleeping and recruiting your strength."

On other nights, Tenzen's words would have been an invitation and Rakurai would have taken them that way.

On this night, Rakurai's heartache and his own worries distracted them both.

With passion and sleep equally far from his mind, Tenzen pulled Rakurai's head onto his shoulder, relieved when Rakurai curled in close. Their fingers tangled, and the kisses they shared were comfort, assurance, and declaration.

Tenzen feared that Daisuke, Gedele, or whoever did their bidding had set a trap for Rakurai. And he resolved not to let Rakurai out of his sight—even if it earned him another punishment.

Double Impact

"Set up a shrine as soon as you arrive." Tenzen drew a brush through Rakurai's silver hair. The night hadn't changed his lover's determination, though his zeal burned a little less brightly, as if he'd made himself consider what his actions might cost him and hadn't liked the results.

Tenzen had spent the hours while he held Rakurai visualising the site of the Yuvines' Solstice Council. Dimmuborgir, a collapsed lava dome resembling a ruined castle, was an impressive location for a council meeting. Its crumbling towers, walls, and unexpected open spaces also made it a perfect place for an ambush.

He thinned the veil, so Rakurai had a chance to see the terrain for himself. "I can sense only a handful of Yuvine in the area. Nowhere near enough for a council meeting."

"It's a day yet to the solstice. I'm sure the elders won't want to while away a few hours over a picnic and small talk." Rakurai scrutinised the jumble of rocks and brush with a fighter's keen gaze.

"What if your elders don't turn up?"

"Then I won't be able to warn them that our two worlds are in danger." He took Tenzen's hands, holding tight as if he needed the support. "Please understand. I can't let it be said that a Yamakage shirks his duty. Or that I ignore a call from the Council of Elders. All my choices impact Raijin. I won't let them fashion something as minor as attendance at a meeting into a whip to beat him with."

"You're willing to risk your life for... your reputation?"

"For Raijin's safety. To ensure that he'll be treated as he deserves and not be made to suffer for my choices."

Tenzen conceded defeat. He didn't relish conflict. It was one reason he'd kept to himself and hadn't looked far beyond his garden and the souls he protected. All the Shinigami shared this trait to varying degrees, but instead of peaceful cooperation, they'd only succeeded in bringing danger and strife to their gardens.

Rakurai was different. He didn't choose between peace and war. Rakurai chose between what he perceived as right or wrong. Facing an ambush seemed a small price to pay for doing right. Not that his choice made him happy.

It didn't make Tenzen happy, either. But at least he could watch over Rakurai and Raijin and help when help was needed.

He set down the brush and Rakurai turned and looped his arms around Tenzen's neck. A small frown hovered between his brows. "Thanks to you, I'm prepared for an ambush. But if there is a chance to meet with the Council of Elders and warn them, then I must take it. I would be remiss in my duties if I did not."

"I know. And I understand, even if I don't like it." He pulled Rakurai close and kissed him, putting all his love, his anguish, and the assurances he couldn't speak into the touch of lips and tongues.

"Your first task is to stay alive, so you can return to Raijin and to me." Tenzen waited until Rakurai had buckled on his sword and pushed the whips through their loops on his belt. "Do not close yourself off from me," he warned. "I'll not accept it."

It shocked him out of his dark mood when Rakurai barked out a laugh. "Your company has given me joy since the day we met. I would never forsake that, even if I knew how to go about it. Which, I'm happy to say, I don't."

Rakurai stepped from Tenzen's arms into a ring of stones and couldn't hold back his chuckle. Tenzen rarely asked anything for himself, but when he wanted something badly enough, he wasn't subtle about making it happen.

He took off his amulet and set it on the ground. It glittered in a flash of black light, so swift that Rakurai wasn't sure he'd seen it until a tingle of power shot up his fingertips.

"Tenzen," he murmured. "I love you. I adore you. I worship you. And I beg you to watch over Raijin." He never asked protection for himself. Asking protection for Raijin was just as unnecessary, yet he did it every time. Mortals, even long-lived Yuvine, were irrational like that.

He straightened and the shard of obsidian became a piece of rock amongst rocks, utterly at home in this eerie place.

It's like standing in a cave, Rakurai marvelled. *The walls curve up and in as if trying to join over my head.* He ran his fingers over the rock: pitted, cracked, and razor-sharp in some places, glassy smooth obsidian in others.

You're standing in a bubble forged from lava and steam, Tenzen said.

He'd seen Dimmuborgir birthed, Rakurai knew. He'd witnessed the flood of lava roll over the lake, had watched steam shape it into a dome that shattered into the fantastical, jagged shapes Rakurai beheld now. The intervening two thousand years had allowed the ground to cool, and moss, grass, and a few shrubby trees to take hold. They hadn't lessened the feeling of something born from primordial violence. Neither did the silence all around him.

I could be the only one alive on earth.

You're not. Anger laced Tenzen's voice. *I sense six others close to your position, and a few more a little further away.*

The Solstice Council?

The traditional meeting place lies empty.

Rakurai didn't doubt that it would stay that way. He'd wanted Tenzen to be wrong. He couldn't imagine eleven hunters turning assassin and attacking one of their own. But even as he argued he'd known better. Already his neck was tight, and his shoulder blades itched as if he wore a target on his back.

Resigned to a game of hide and seek, Rakurai took stock of the terrain.

Jagged columns and walls of sharp-edged basalt provided cover while interrupting his lines of sight. Loose ash and pumice made for tricky footing. And sounds would carry in the near-oppressive silence.

Even covered in dull, reddish dust, his white haori blazed like a beacon. Rakurai slipped it off his shoulders, giving himself a better chance to melt into the background. Then he tugged the short whip from his belt and let the cord uncoil before he gathered it loosely.

He knew that the Solstice Council met twice a year in the large clearing at the centre of the former lava dome. Open, airy, and with level footing, it made for an ideal debating space and offered plenty of room for the leaders of the twelve clans to gather. Rakurai was the Yamakage clan's designated hunter, but he'd attended few council meetings here. It left him at a disadvantage.

Anyone close by? he asked as he approached one opening in the rugged wall and peered out, only to find more walls and pillars of jagged rocks on the other side.

Two on the other side of the clearing. They're not aware of your presence.

Then I should make haste and announce myself. Rakurai stepped into a patch of loose stones, the crunch loud in the silence.

You have their attention.

Excellent. Rakurai headed off, not in the direction Tenzen had indicated, but back across his little almost-cave and through the gap on the opposite side of the wall. He needed to get his bearings. If he could draw out the opposition—and prove that they *were* his enemies—while he did so, then so much the better.

Not even the air stirred inside the broken dome. Grey clouds hung thick and low, adding to the oppressive stillness that magnified even the slightest rustle of cloth into position-revealing sound. Rakurai circled the location of the two Yuvine, then took a gamble and jumped to the top of one of the rocky towers, hoping for a lack of loose material underfoot. His boots met soft moss and he breathed out before he straightened to survey the site from his new vantage point.

Four at your back, two in front of you, Tenzen informed him.

There's no reason to assume they wish me ill.

Don't lie to yourself. Don't lie to me, either.

Let's test the assumption then. Rakurai jumped from his tower of rock and landed five feet in front of the two Yuvine.

A heartbeat later he had his answer.

He dodged one thrown blade and lost strands of hair to a second before he regained his feet. Despite their size, power, and claws, demons were easier to fight than trained Yuvine hunters. Especially when both came at him at once. Rakurai's whip knocked one off his feet while he traded blows with the other.

Metal rang on metal, and Rakurai had no illusions about what was to come.

They know you're here now, Tenzen confirmed. *And the next lot's about to cut you off.*

Boots crunched on stone somewhere to Rakurai's right. He swung his whip, forcing his two attackers back. Then he turned and sprinted across the clearing.

He barely made it.

Two hunters followed him through the break in the crumbling wall. They raced across the circle, eyes on the gap on the opposite side. Neither spotted the obsidian pendant on the ground, either before or after a boot had sent it flying.

Rakurai had never seen a death god in a rage.

Taller, broader, and more overwhelming, Tenzen burst through the veil and grabbed the nearest hunter by the throat. Without effort he slung him into the wall and Rakurai heard the man's neck crack. The light died from his eyes a moment later.

Tenzen let him crumple to the ground. He turned to Rakurai next, the only other living soul trapped with him in the enclosed circle, but his gaze softened, and he didn't reach out to do damage.

Instead, he jumped over the wall as if fifteen feet were nothing and landed on the other side.

Rakurai ran after him, not wanting to let Tenzen face the attackers alone, until it occurred to him how ridiculous that notion was. Tenzen was a god in a rage and Rakurai would do well to stay out of his way.

The sounds of Tenzen's rampage filled the dome and Rakurai, lost in admiration, almost missed the soft scrape of a boot that betrayed an approach. Whip at the ready, he turned and—

"Adel?" Rakurai had trained with the Egyptian hunter while they served in the Custodia. They'd even spent leisure time together.

"Yamakage." Harun Adel gave an ironic bow before he dropped into a fighting stance.

Rakurai kept his whip steady. "Why are you doing this?"

"Orders."

"Whose?"

Harun grimaced and shifted his stance. "You wouldn't believe me if I told you."

"Try me."

Harun opened his mouth and—

A knife flashed through the air. It thudded into Harun's back, cutting off anything he might have said.

Harun pitched forward before Rakurai could reach him, gaze already lifeless.

Rakurai hit the ground and rolled.

Not fast enough.

The second blade found him as securely as the first had found Harun's back.

Heat lanced through him, sharper than a lightning bolt. It knocked the air from his lungs and—for one fear-filled instant—left him unable to breathe. Digging his nails into his palm until the tiny, insignificant ache registered cut through the panic. He stayed where he was, muscles coiled, waiting for the assassin to come and finish what he'd started.

Nothing happened.

Rakurai sucked air in short, shallow breaths that burned like fire. Had Harun been condemned to die, or had he been killed so he couldn't answer Rakurai's question?

Gritting his teeth, Rakurai yanked the knife from his side. He ignored the pain, the bleeding wound, and Harun's corpse.

And followed the killer.

He spotted him behind an outcrop of rock when a scream rent the air. Shrill and terrified, it came from right across the clearing, and Rakurai had only one thought: Tenzen!

He sent a bolt of lightning into the nearest wall, upending tons of rock on top of Harun's killer, steeled himself, and ran.

Tenzen didn't need his help. He stood at the centre of a group of dead hunters, eyes wild, and robe splattered with blood. Judging by the state of his hands, he hadn't bothered to use a weapon.

"Are there any more?"

Tenzen blinked himself back to the present. "No," he said, voice deep and scratchy. "That's everyone who's here. And no Solstice Council."

Rakurai bowed his head. "You were right. And I was a fool to hope."

"Hope is never foolish." Tenzen stretched out a hand, then drew it back, frowning at the blood. He wiped his palms on his robe, leaving long, red smears on the white fabric, before he repeated the gesture, and waited for the souls of the dead Yuvine to alight on his palm.

They came, one by one, and Rakurai—fascinated as always by the spectacle—counted them as they settled. "Twelve."

"Twelve," Tenzen agreed.

Twelve assassins. Twelve Yuvine clans. Rakurai's breath caught as that detail registered. He took two quick steps, planning to check the dead Yuvine for—

His knees buckled and he hissed in pain as he went down, hand going to his wound.

"What is it? Are you hurt?" Tenzen was beside him in an instant, tearing through Rakurai's robe to inspect the injury.

"A knife." Rakurai tried to make light. "I need to—"

"You need to come to my garden," Tenzen said in a tone that brooked no argument. "You're losing too much blood." He lifted his hands from the wound.

When Rakurai beheld the sodden rags that had been his robe, he couldn't but agree.

Claiming

"Why your garden?" Rakurai asked as Tenzen shepherded him through the gate and into a meadow of tall grasses and wildflowers.

Rakurai's first appreciative breath of the warm, scented air turned into an agonised fit of coughing, and he clung to Tenzen's arm. Blood loss made him dizzy, and pain throbbed in his bones with every stubborn step. But neither pain nor dizziness were a match for the thirst that plagued him. If he'd had to come to the Otherworld, he much preferred it to have been Tenzen's home.

"Why your garden?" he asked again.

"You need to heal. If you want to confront your clan elder, you need to be whole. Lie down."

A stone bench had appeared out of nowhere, and Rakurai sank onto it. "I hadn't planned to confront Daisuke."

"This has to end, Rakurai. Truly. Your elders have lost their way."

Rakurai took the cup Tenzen handed him and drained it thirstily. Tenzen refilled it. Not with water this time. The liquid tasted of herbs and burned Rakurai's throat on the way down. But it eased the light-headedness.

"Lie down. Let the potion and my garden get to work."

Tenzen took a seat at the end of the bench and Rakurai stretched out as bidden, his head pillowed on Tenzen's thigh.

He hadn't really thought this through, he realised. He'd wanted to help Tenzen protect their worlds, not cut ties with his clan. "I'm not sure I'm ready for this."

"How can you not be ready? Your patience really is the stuff of legends!"

Rakurai surged upright, but Tenzen pushed him back. "Stay down. Let your wound heal. Maybe we should discuss this later."

"No. I've been as wilfully blind as you've claimed to be, Tenzen. I'd resigned myself to these clumsy attacks when I should have done something about them a long time ago. At the very least, I should have made sure it *was* Daisuke trying to remove me and tried to learn the reason."

"You didn't believe Daisuke—or anyone else—would dare to break Jumon's rules in this way. You trusted that they all had as much honour as you do."

The touch of Tenzen's fingers combing through his hair soothed his agitation. It didn't soothe the heartache. "Do you realise that we've just decimated the Custodia? We killed the whole contingent of designated hunters, Tenzen! In one afternoon, I've done more damage to the Yuvine than Daisuke has in his lifetime."

"I doubt that. I've not yet tallied Gedele and Daisuke's body count, but we know that both Tan Hao and Vigdis take their orders from Gedele. Remember the rafeet that attacked us on the bridge outside the archive? Vigdis Perkhon set them on your trail."

"Are you sure?" Rakurai started to argue. "You said rafeet lose their memories and—"

"I'm certain. Their souls are in my garden. They've lost their memories of being reborn as rafeet. They remember their lives in the Otherworld just fine."

Rakurai's spurt of temper died away. Given what they'd found in the archives, Tenzen's news shouldn't have come as a surprise. So why did he feel so shaken? "If I confront Daisuke, I'll be cutting ties with my clan. Forsaking the Yuvine."

"You're loyal to people who don't offer you loyalty in return, Rakurai. What if Daisuke or Tan Hao one day order Raijin to kill you?"

Rakurai turned his head away, but Tenzen didn't let him off the hook. "Can you guarantee that they won't?"

"That's not what I'm worried about," Rakurai admitted. "If they ever put Raijin in that position, I'm certain he'll do what's right. What worries me is that they might attack him to punish me. I can't bear the thought of putting Raijin in danger."

"Your son is a capable fighter."

"But I've never shared any of my misgivings with him. I've not even told him yet about Gedele and Daisuke targeting Yuvine interested in witchcraft. We never discussed clan politics in his hearing. Naomi and I decided not to taint his choices and I stuck to it, all these years. I thought there'd be time to talk when he was grown. It seems foolish now."

"Rakurai, listen to me. You may have kept your opinions to yourself, but Raijin's been watching you. He's following the example you set. You didn't shut him away from the world, either. He's met plenty of people growing up, and he isn't as easy to sway as you may think. Besides…"

Rakurai waited, but Tenzen didn't continue. When he cast a look upwards, he saw speculation on Tenzen's face.

"Besides what?"

"I wish we knew why someone wants you dead. Without that knowledge, all we can do is speculate."

"What are you thinking?"

"That you're a skilled hunter. You wield power, knowledge, and lightning. Part of me thinks that you're standing in someone's way. The other part of me… Well… you forsaking your clan will cause a great deal of talk. It may lead other Yuvine to examine their choices. It might also deflect attention from Raijin."

"It might do that. Still…" Rakurai sighed. He couldn't see the future. He could only do his best and hope.

"The Yuvine have reached the end of their road. Forsaking their gifts, compromising the safety of two worlds, killing each other… They're breaking the agreement and the Unseen Power won't tolerate that for long."

Tenzen was deadly serious and Rakurai's heart ached more than the healing wound in his side. How had events escalated so quickly? He'd hoped to have more time with Raijin. Now he was out of time and options.

Tenzen was right, though. The ambush had proven that Rakurai had all the Yuvine against him.

But he had a Shinigami by his side.

He reached for Tenzen's hand and twined their fingers. He let the firm grip steady him, and tried to prepare himself for a confrontation with Yamakage Daisuke.

Returning home had been bittersweet. Finding that Raijin had gone up the mountain to train and knowing he couldn't wait for him to return was just bitter.

Rakurai had hoped for a chance to have that long-postponed conversation. He'd wanted to remind Raijin to be careful, and not to believe everything Daisuke, Tan Hao, or any Yuvine clan elders told him. Most of all, he'd wanted to make sure Raijin understood how much he meant to Rakurai, and that he'd always be there for him should he have need.

In the end, he decided to write.

The moon bathed the garden in silver light when Rakurai finally set the brush down. He'd laboured for hours over his letter, composing and discarding thought after thought and sentence after sentence, until he was sure he'd expressed himself in terms that couldn't be misread.

Rakurai needed Raijin to know that necessity—not choice—had prompted his disappearance. And that he would always watch over his son.

As he shook sand over Raijin's name, carefully inked on the front of the folded paper, he could no longer keep the moisture from his lashes. His breath grew ragged, as if he had performed a massive labour, and he felt an impulse to tear up his writing, find Raijin and make him join them in the Otherworld.

When the veil opened and Tenzen appeared beside the doors leading into the garden, Rakurai had never been more grateful. He set Raijin's letter on top of his pack, then crossed the room to bury his sorrow in Tenzen's arms for a few moments of respite.

Despite the late hour, the Yamakage clan house was brightly lit, inside and out. Tenzen scanned the area, checking for traps and ambushes and wishing that he could take on the Yamakage in Rakurai's stead.

"There are surprisingly few servants about for a house that looks as if it is hosting a major party."

"Daisuke has never learned the meaning of the word restraint." Rakurai straightened his obi belt. His wound was healed, but he was pale, and strain drew thin lines around his mouth. "I'd better do this."

"You will be protected."

Rakurai managed a smile before he stepped through the veil and out of Tenzen's reach.

Tenzen stayed close to Rakurai, just on the other side of the veil and invisible to anyone in the human realm, as Rakurai approached the entrance.

"I wish to see Elder Daisuke," he said.

The steward bowed as if Rakurai had been expected. "Please follow me."

Tenzen kept step with Rakurai as they moved from the genkan deeper into the house. The council chamber was a large, high-ceilinged room, turned sombre even on the brightest day by a dark wooden floor and panelled walls.

It wasn't sombre or gloomy then. The huge chandelier had been lowered from the exposed roof beams, and every single light on it blazed brightly.

The seventeen members of the Yamakage clan council sat on silk cushions, each beside a low writing desk of black cedar inlaid with gold. They were dressed in their most formal robes, and each turned their eyes towards the opening doors.

They didn't expect to see you.

And just look at their faces. They're each as guilty as the other.

Rakurai didn't wait to be announced. He strode into the council chamber and didn't bother with even a cursory bow. "I wish to know," he addressed Daisuke, "why you had me ambushed at the meeting place of the Solstice Council."

The Yamakage elder drew himself up. "I gave no such order."

"No?" Rakurai's tone was a challenge, and a few of the elders grew pale.

Tenzen noted each one.

"Commander Tan Hao took his orders from Elder Gedele Perkhon," Rakurai said. "He called on each clan's designated hunters and sent them after me. And you yourself ordered Yamakage Hideki to join them. I didn't need to come here to learn any of that."

He spoke nothing but the truth. Tenzen had got all that and more from the dead assassins' souls.

"Then why did you come? You never bothered yourself about clan affairs. What is it that is suddenly so urgent?"

"If I haven't shown any interest in playing at politics, it is because my time was better spent elsewhere."

"No doubt," Daitō sneered from his place at one end of the semi-circle. Tenzen thought it was a surprisingly good approximation of Daisuke's habitual expression. "We all know about your lover in the Otherworld."

"Do you now?" Rakurai's voice turned silky. "What is it, exactly, that you think you know about my private life?"

"I know," the younger man aped Rakurai's words, "that you spend more time in the Otherworld than in the human realm. I know that you show no care for your clan, or your family. I know that you're a perverted piece of—"

"That's enough!" Daisuke rose from his seat. He didn't even glance at his nephew. All his attention was on Rakurai. "What happened to the hunters?"

"The assassins, you mean? What usually happens to such men. They died to further your ambitions." Rakurai watched Daisuke draw a breath and spoke before the other man could. "Yes, Hideki is dead, too."

"Hideki was…"

"Barely of age. You had no right—"

"You killed him."

"I will kill anyone who attacks me."

"Those men were loyal hunters."

Tenzen seethed at the implication. He wanted... He wanted to show Rakurai that he wasn't alone. He wanted to make sure the elders of his clan understood that, too.

And then he realised that he could do just that.

He opened the veil and stood in the gash, watching everything from under lowered lashes.

Whispers swept the council chamber, but nobody dared interrupt Daisuke and Rakurai, even while they studied Tenzen with curious eyes.

"Yes, the hunters you sent after me were loyal. And you repaid their loyalty with lies. That, Elder Daisuke, is what I came here to say. I went to the Solstice Council to warn the Yuvine elders that both our worlds are in danger. That our defences grow thin because the Yuvine are not keeping to the terms of Jumon's agreement with the Unseen Power. I came to warn you and you sent assassins after me. Would you care to tell the esteemed councillors why you did so?"

"The real reason," Tenzen added quietly, sensing Daisuke's intent to evade the question with another attack on Rakurai. "Tell them the reason Gedele Perkhon shared with you. And then justify the choice you made."

"I owe you no explanation," Daisuke began.

Tenzen raised his head.

Shock rippled through the hall. Silks rustled as every council member prostrated himself. Yamakage Daisuke was the last to kneel, and the stiffness in his shoulders showed how much he resented the need to do so.

"Explain your reasons for breaking Jumon's rules," Tenzen demanded. "Or face my wrath."

Daisuke sat up. He kept his eyes lowered while he sought an answer that wouldn't condemn him.

Tenzen knew he wouldn't find one. He'd allowed the Yuvine to neglect their duty. And he'd conspired to cause the death of other Yuvine.

"It's all a plot!" Daitō shouted suddenly, jumping to his feet. "Don't be deceived. This is no god! It's a plot hatched by Rakurai and his lover. I'll not stand by and—" A slim knife flew from his fingers.

Rakurai threw himself in front of Tenzen, presenting his unprotected back.

Tenzen's hand flashed out.

Through the veil.

Around Rakurai.

And the blade pierced his palm.

Tenzen glared. How dare they try to kill Rakurai right in front of him! Fury darkened his vision as he pulled the knife from his hand. "Dishonourable." He touched the blade to his lips. "And poison. You will regret this. I swear—"

"Tenzen, no!" Rakurai could have joined Tenzen in the Otherworld. He could have reached through the veil, touched Tenzen's hand to soothe his anger. He could have tried to distract Tenzen in a number of ways.

He did the one thing Tenzen hadn't expected. He sank to his knees and bowed his head. "Please, Tenzen. I beg you. Don't punish all the Yamakage for the ill-considered actions of one."

It hung in the balance. Tenzen's need for revenge pitted against Rakurai's plea. Then Tenzen chuckled, a rasp made from knife blades and shards of glass. "You underestimate how much I value you, Rakurai," he rumbled. "I wasn't about to swear vengeance on the Yamakage. I was about to swear vengeance on all Yuvine. Because they all banded together to punish you for choosing honour over expediency. Stand."

Rakurai rose and Tenzen clasped his hand, turned him so that he seemed to stand side-by-side with the Shinigami, though Tenzen had not set one foot into the human realm. Before them, the councillors lay prostrate, sweating and shaking.

As they should.

"I claim this man, Yamakage Rakurai, and all of his family as my own," Tenzen spoke into the tense silence. "Any harm done to any of them will be harm done to me and punished as such. Do you understand me?"

Murmurs of agreement came in answer, but Tenzen wasn't yet satisfied.

"As for you," he pointed at Daisuke's nephew. "You have dishonoured yourself and your clan. You will face the consequences of your actions." He felt Rakurai twitch beside him and squeezed his hand. "You will live," he said, not taking his eyes from the prostrate man, "but you will experience what you had in store for Rakurai." He flicked the knife across the room, watching as it embedded itself in Daitō's arm. Had the knife hit Rakurai—without Tenzen or his garden nearby—he'd have died in excruciating pain. "For every day of your natural life."

Daitō's scream turned into a pain-filled whimper as he yanked out the knife and curled into himself. It was fear rather than actual pain at that point, Tenzen knew, but he didn't want Rakurai to be present when the real screaming started. He didn't think any of the Yamakage present would be compassionate enough to help Daitō then.

Self-interest, envy, vanity, and greed fought for dominance in the councillor's minds and Tenzen itched to remove Rakurai from their orbit. He wanted Rakurai in his home, his bed, his garden… but with the threat of Tenzen's wrath hanging over the clan, Rakurai didn't have to leave the human realm. He could spend more time with Raijin, could even accompany him to the Custodia.

Daisuke wouldn't raise a hand against either Rakurai or his son. He wouldn't dare. And neither would any other Yuvine.

Rakurai had every reason to stay in the human realm, and Tenzen had little enough to tempt him to leave. He held Rakurai's letter out to him and waited for Rakurai to make his choice.

Rakurai's gaze rested on the letter in his hand. He moved to pocket it, then hesitated and cast one long look around the council chamber.

Tenzen couldn't breathe. He wanted to step through the veil and pull Rakurai into his arms. He wanted to wipe the scheming councillors from the face of the earth. He wanted...

He wanted more than he'd ever asked for in all his years, but he also knew that the choice had to be Rakurai's.

He stood watchful and unmoving, reminding himself over and over that Rakurai wouldn't be lost to him, even if he chose to remain in the human realm. They'd speak. They'd continue to meet. And whatever happened between them, his lonely existence was a thing of the past.

"Unlike you, I keep my word," Rakurai said suddenly. "And I've sworn to fulfil the clan's obligations." He held out the letter, waiting for Daisuke to take it.

"You will give this note, unopened, into Yamakage Raijin's hand," Tenzen ordered, when the man didn't move.

"Yes, Kami-sama," Daisuke mumbled. He glowered, but he would ensure the letter reached Rakurai's son. Or Tenzen would do it for him.

"Rethink your adherence to Jumon's rules," Tenzen said. "Or you may find yourself presiding over the end of the Yuvine."

He widened the gash in the veil and stood aside. And after one final look at Daisuke and the letter he clutched in his fingers, Rakurai joined him in the Otherworld.

Six Months Later

Gedele Perkhon stepped through the veil into knee-deep snow. The cold bit at her bare face and hands and she wrapped her arms around herself and wished for a thicker cloak. Three days in Egypt had been enough to make her gasp at the biting cold of a Latvian winter.

Around her, firs and larches stretched their snowy crowns towards a leaden sky, and the colour of the clouds told her that another snowfall was imminent. It was fortunate that she knew these woods, or the approaching dusk and the overcast sky would have made orienting herself difficult.

She'd meant to arrive near her house, but travel through the veil had become unreliable of late. There'd been instances when she'd arrived at her destination not heartbeats after leaving her home but hours later, even though she hadn't tarried in the Otherworld. And now it seemed that arriving in the right location was becoming a problem too.

Gedele tucked the hem of her skirt into her belt and worked her way out of the drift. She was the second oldest Yuvine, and the most powerful, yet she had no wish to spend the night out in the open. She wouldn't die but didn't want to risk frostbite either.

Pondering the riddle of the veil served as a distraction while she fought her way through the deep snow. For fourteen hundred years, she'd passed through the veil easily and without mishap. But many things were going wrong lately, and the idiosyncrasies of travelling through the Otherworld were just one more.

It's more of a nuisance, she decided, picking her way through the trees. *Tan Hao's blunder was so much worse.*

Instead of fomenting unrest in the Yamakage clan as she'd asked him to, Tan Hao had set an ambush for Rakurai Yamakage. And Rakurai had taken no prisoners. The massacre had been a blow. She'd been thousands of miles away when the hunters died and she grieved, not for the hunters lost but for the loss of the celestial magic each of them had borne in their souls.

It was a waste the Yuvine couldn't afford.

"A waste *I* can't afford!"

As for the Yamakage… she didn't believe a word of Daisuke's fear-soaked blubbering. Threatened by a death god, indeed! Though she couldn't deny that Rakurai had vanished. And that twelve hunters had died in Dimmuborgir.

At least her visit to Egypt had offered her comfort. Yes, Samala Adel, the Egyptian clan elder, had asked uncomfortable questions about their hunter's death. Their clan's seer had determined that Harun had been killed—not by the landslide Tan Hao had blamed for the disaster—but by a hunter from the Tibetan clan. But Gedele had been able to divert their attentions, suggesting that there might have been a feud between the Tibetan and Harun, however unlikely it seemed.

After a while Samala had stopped asking questions. Harun's loss was a matter of concern to him, but not the reason he'd called for Gedele. He had a family dying from an unknown poison, and needed Gedele's help.

She'd made herself look busy for two long days and when all three died on the third day, she took the opportunity to add to her store of celestial magic. The dead Yuvines' souls moved to the Otherworld. They had no need of that magic, while Gedele never stopped her search for more.

She pulled her cloak closer and sought inside herself for the reservoir of magic at her core. It lay safe and serene, like a pool of water glittering in the moonlight, and Gedele wanted to weep. Adding the innate magic of twelve hunters would have been an unexpected boon, and she grieved for what she now would never have.

Her damp lashes grew heavy as tears turned to ice. She used her sleeve to scrub them clear. She knew better, damn it! And weeping didn't change a thing.

Ahead of her, the forest thinned. Soil and leaves covered the ground, dark against the snowy forest.

Gedele halted at the edge of a snowless circle and stared at the trees.

Every single one was dead.

She couldn't decide what had happened here. In fourteen centuries, she'd experienced plenty of natural disasters. She'd survived fire, water, war, and famine. Yet she'd never seen a clump of dead trees in a patch of snowless earth in the middle of winter.

Had she arrived in the woods, an hour from her home, to see this?

She took a careful step into the circle. Her feet slid in the top layer of mulch and mud, the soil squishing under her boots. She knelt in the dirt and touched her palms to the ground, finding the soil warm and pliable, not frozen as it should have been. And the smell wafting up to her was rank with the aroma of rotten eggs.

Could an underground spring be poisoning the trees?

Once, her rare healing gift would have allowed her to return the trees to life. Today, there was no chance of her even attempting it. Restoring life required an incredible amount of magic, more than was available to her now that the Yuvine world held twelve clans.

Her gift hadn't survived the rise of the third clan, and she'd grieved and raged and researched for decades before she figured out what had happened. She'd been working to reclaim her gift ever since.

Dried needles rained down on her, shaken loose by a sudden gust. The storm was close and Gedele knew she needed to move lest she be caught by the snowfall.

Anger and sadness bloomed in her heart at the sight of the dead trees. Along with a desperate hope. She hadn't attempted to use her gift in centuries. Might now be the right time to revive it?

She touched her fingertips to the bark. Tiny knots and ridges bit into her skin. She breathed out and pressed down harder, felt the jolt when she connected and waited for the tree to seek what it needed.

The draw on her power wasn't gentle. Savage pain wrenched at her insides, tore and clawed at the magic in her core. Gedele screamed in shock. She yanked her fingers away as if they'd been burned and huddled at the base of the tree, sobbing and hugging herself as she had the day her gift had been stolen from her.

The pool of magic in her soul shivered and pulsed and Gedele pushed to her feet and fled the snowless circle and the dying trees as fast at her feet would carry her.

She slowed her terror-filled flight as the edge of her village came into view. Lights glowed in the windows, and she smelled burning wood and roasting meat on the wind. This forest had been her home for centuries, yet she still didn't understand all its mysteries.

Between trees and soil out of alignment with the natural order, demon incursions that had increased in number and severity for no apparent reason, and travel through the veil becoming unreliable, it seemed as if the whole world was stumbling.

Gedele mashed her lips together in a tight, hard line and started walking towards her home once more. She had much work ahead of her if she wanted to unravel all these mysteries while replenishing her core of magic. But Gedele had never shied from work.

"What happened to you?" Rakurai stared in dismay at Tenzen's wet, bedraggled form. Mud smeared his clothes and clumped on his boots. Some of it even streaked his hair. And long, ragged tears exposed the lining of his cloak. "You look as if you ran into another pack of rafeet."

"Accurate. They don't just fight in packs, now. They share information, too. It seems they were waiting for us."

Rakurai squinted at the snow drifting from the clouds in huge, wet flakes. "Wonderful. Are you hurt? Is Okandi?"

"Okandi is fine and headed back to her garden. I'm just wet and dirty. And dreaming of a bath and food."

Rakurai brushed damp tendrils of hair out of his face. "I'm done mopping up here. Half a dozen rafeet and a bunch of smaller demons. I… didn't manage to count those."

"Don't worry. I'll call, they come."

Rakurai watched as Tenzen stretched out a hand, waiting until, one by one, butterflies settled on his palm. He couldn't hear Tenzen's call—if he called—but the sight of the butterflies appearing out of nowhere always cheered him. Even creatures as vile as rafeet possessed souls and Tenzen didn't hesitate to take them in and care for them. Something was wrong with the world when a death god showed more compassion to demons than the Yuvine extended to each other.

"That's all of them," Tenzen said, finally. "And they've not been in the Otherworld for long."

"A new gash in the veil?"

"Possibly. I'll find out what I can tomorrow. For now… shall we head home?"

Rakurai nodded and took Tenzen's hand, convinced he knew where their next steps would lead them.

He wasn't wrong. Two heartbeats later they stood in the bathing area of Tenzen's home. Paper screens shielded the area from the snow falling on the garden. The water in the tub sent billows of steam into the air, and four braziers warmed the small space.

Rakurai couldn't wait to sink into the hot water.

He dropped his muddy clothes, uncaring where they landed, and reached for washcloth and soap. Shivering in the chill, he scrubbed himself clean, not surprised when Tenzen stood ready with a bucket of hot water to help him rinse off the soap.

"Go soak," Tenzen instructed when Rakurai was free of suds.

"You said exactly that the first time you brought me here."

Tenzen's smile was soft and beautiful. "I'm determined to say it until the ends of time. It's my first and best reminder that I'm no longer alone."

Rakurai blinked, unable to find a reply. Tenzen had a knack for reducing him to incoherence, even if it most often happened when they shared a sleeping mat.

"Go soak," Tenzen said again. "There's food if you want it."

Of course, there was. A tray holding both their favourite snacks had appeared on the edge of the soaking tub, and alongside it sat two ceramic bottles of sake.

"It hasn't been that bad a day," Rakurai said as he settled into the hot water and took a first sip of his sake. His mouth filled with the flavour of pears, and he raised his brows in surprise. "That's... unusual."

"A gift from Okandi. She thought you might like it." Tenzen finished rinsing his hair and joined Rakurai in the soaking tub. "And you seemed in need of something stronger than tea. What bothers you?"

"That we fight eight days out of every ten, and there are still no Yuvine joining us?"

Tenzen touched his side, where the knife wound he'd received in Dimmuborgir had left a thin scar. "We killed twelve hunters. It will take time for the Custodia to rebuild."

Rakurai hoped Tenzen was right. He wanted a chance to see his son again.

"He's safe," Tenzen said, reading his mood as he often did. "He's up on the plateau, honing his lightning. Word of my threat has spread to all Yuvine clans. Nobody will dare touch him."

Rakurai laced their fingers together in silent gratitude. Tenzen didn't question his need to watch over Raijin. He often thinned the veil for Rakurai to catch sight of his son. More than anything, Rakurai wanted to visit. He'd always dreamed of accompanying Raijin to the Custodia. But Daisuke had Raijin watched and Raijin never gave a sign that he missed his father.

"He still hasn't given Raijin your letter," Tenzen said.

"And Raijin will head to Capri in a month."

"Maybe I need to—"

"Don't. Daisuke can teach lessons in spite. I don't want either of you exposed to his malice."

Tenzen chuckled. "You realise that he can't touch me."

"Not physically, no. But words can sting, too. And," he forged on doggedly. "I'm coming to realise that I've never really given Raijin his due. He knows his own mind and makes his own choices."

"He's had you as his father."

"What I mean is… whether Daisuke gives him my letter or not, Raijin knows me. I hope he knows all the things I put in my letter without needing to read it."

Tenzen refilled their sake cups and held Rakurai's out to him. "Which reminds me. Did I tell you how Tan Hao tried to explain twelve dead hunters?"

"No."

"An avalanche."

"On summer solstice?"

"Quite. According to Okandi, Gedele just looked at him until he decided to use a landslide as an excuse."

Rakurai had met the eldest Shinigami after joining Tenzen in the Otherworld. She was irreverent and outspoken, and Rakurai was glad she'd offered to keep an eye on Yuvine activities in the human realm. Having to watch Daisuke, Tan Hao, Gedele and the rest play at politics as if nothing was at stake would have riled him to violence. When he already had plenty of violence in his days.

"The souls of the dead demons," he began, "do they ever have a chance at a normal life?"

"A human one, you mean?" Tenzen considered that. He floated in the bath with his head resting against the padded rim, his eyes closed, and his dark hair trailing in the water. And he appeared so much like home that Rakurai was no longer interested in hearing an answer.

"Let's not worry about this right now," he suggested, sliding closer and trailing his fingertips over Tenzen's chest. "I'm sure we can come back to it later."

Tenzen arched into the touch and turned his head for a kiss. "Of course, we can. But your question is easy to answer. Provided they are patient, every creature gets a chance at a normal life. Even an immortal death god."

THANK YOU!

Thank you for reading Caught. I am the Tiger, Guardian of Manuscripts and Office Chairs.

As you can see, I'm hard at work making Jackie finish Cursed, the next book in the series, and I could really do with a treat from the special drawer. Every time someone leaves a review, I get one of those, so... please?

Don't go away just yet... I've convinced Jackie to show off the cover for Cursed, which will be out soon.

If you would like to read along while Jackie writes and get all her books delivered to your inbox a week before they go on sale, you can become a patron. And if you want more pictures of me, and recipes, snippets, and stories, make sure you visit Jackie's Kitchen on Facebook.

Raijin killed a witch and found himself cursed.

Sandro went to Raijin's aid and became an assassin's target.

Neither expected to find himself at the centre of the biggest upheaval their world had seen in a thousand years.

And that it was the love between them that would win the day and lift the curse.

Cursed, the second book in the Balance of Magic series, is a slow-burn m/m fantasy romance featuring friends-to-lovers who become soulmates, irate death gods, curses, inept, narcissistic politicians, curious, compassionate witches, and a found family.

HEALING GLASS

A Gifted Guilds Novel

A dying city.
An ancient, forgotten accord.
And two gifted men caught in a web of greed and dark magic.

Despite belonging to different guilds, glass master Minel and warrior captain Falcon are friends. Their duties keep them apart, but when Minel falls ill and chooses death rather than the only known cure, nothing can keep Falcon from his side.

As their friendship grows into more, old wrongs and one man's machinations threaten the floating city and leave both Minel and Falcon fighting for their lives. Can they learn to combine their gifts to save the city and its magic, or will everything they know and love perish before their eyes?

SWORD OATH

Dornost Saga Tales
Shades Book 1

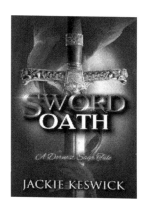

I'll die for you, or with you.

When Madan swore a sword oath to Serrai he was eight years old. He kept his promise while they grew to manhood and took their respective positions as king and general, even when it seemed that he was the only one fated to love, deeply and devotedly.

Serrai never declared his feelings, but his love for Madan was just as fierce. And quietly, in his heart, he swore his own sword oath: to die with Madan.

Until a battlefield death leaves both oaths broken, and two men fighting for a future that doesn't see them forever parted.

SHADOW REALM

Dornost Saga Tales
Shades Book 2

Their love has defeated death. Can it defeat malice and madness?

Serrai and Madan sacrificed their lives for each other, but the quiet afterlife they'd imagined doesn't exist. The Shadow Realm is at war and when the conflict threatens the human world, the Fates demand their help.

Hunting down four renegade Shades and surviving on different sides of the veil between worlds needs courage, stubbornness and strength of will.

Can Madan triumph over hunger, madness, and his own compassion to make it back to Serrai? Can Serrai vanquish jealousy and doubt to hold the gate long enough for Madan to return?

Or will they end forever parted?

REPEAT OFFENCE

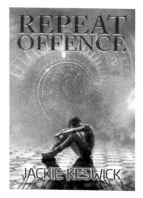

It should have ended with their deaths. But dying in a wash of blood was just the beginning.

Sentenced to eternal life for sacrificing themselves in battle, warriors Taz and Hiro must take turns living as human and Guardian on opposing sides of the veil with only a chance to catch a glance of each other in the moment of death.

Until an attack forces Taz and Hiro to make a choice. Should they cling to what little solace they've carved out for themselves? Or should they sacrifice their lives to save countless others and risk the wrath of the Judges for a second time?

For an emotional, heart-wrenching read, buy Repeat Offence now and follow Taz and Hiro as they fight for a chance to be together!

BAUBLES

Baubles

JACKIE KESWICK

It wasn't the flashiest bauble in the shop, or the largest, but Rica treasured it more than anything else she'd ever made.

Every year, it was the only one left unsold. And every year, Rica packed it carefully away, hoping that, one day, someone would be drawn to this particular piece of glass and magic and would come to claim it.

She'd almost lost that hope, when a stranger walked into her store.

A holiday short story of conviction, hope, and magic.

Meet Jackie

Jackie Keswick was born behind the Iron Curtain with itchy feet, a bent for rocks and a recurring dream of stepping off a bus in the middle of nowhere to go home. She's worked in a hospital and as the only girl with 52 men on an oil rig, spent a winter in Moscow and a summer in Iceland and finally settled in the country of her dreams with her dream team: a husband, a cat, a tandem, and a laptop.

Jackie writes across genres, loves unexpected reunions and second chances, and men who write their own rules. She blogs about English history and food, has a thing for green eyes, and is a great believer in making up soundtracks for everything, including her characters and the cat.

And she still hasn't found the place where the bus stops.

For questions and comments, not restricted to green eyes, bus stops or recipes for traditional English food, you can find her in Jackie's Kitchen, her Facebook readers group, and in all the usual places:

Printed in Great Britain
by Amazon